HOW
I LEARNED
TO HATE IN
OHIO

HOW I LEARNED TO HATE IN OHIO

DAVID STUART MACLEAN

The Overlook Press, New York

Published in 2022 by The Overlook Press, an imprint of ABRAMS.
Originally published in hardcover by The Overlook Press in 2021.

Library of Congress Control Number: 2021934849

Paperback ISBN: 978-1-4197-4720-5

eISBN: 978-1-68335-995-1

Printed and bound in the United States

10 9 8 7 6 5 4 3 2 1

Abrams books are available at special discounts when purchased
in quantity for premiums and promotions as well as fundraising
or educational use. Special editions can also be created to
specification. For details, contact specialsales@abramsbooks.com
or the address below.

ABRAMS The Art of Books
195 Broadway, New York, NY 10007
abramsbooks.com

for Emily

FIRST PART

"Blessed are the weak who think they are
good because they have no claws."
—Baruch Spinoza

CHAPTER 1

My parents bought an old farmhouse when we moved here. It's ancient. Built in 1876 with the weird brownout wiring to prove it. You buy a house this old, you're a person happy to inherit problems, which is fine for the owners—screw them, right? They deserve the problems: the crappy furnace, the inefficient ventilation, the wasps in the attic. It's less enviable for the kids of those people. No one knows what we deserve.

I was the farthest kid out on the bus route. You would think that since I was the first kid picked up that I would have my choice of seats. But thinking that shows you're a fool. There is never a blank slate in a town this size. Or any town. Or anywhere. Live anywhere long enough and you become a person happy to inherit your own problems.

I had a socially assigned seat. Third row from the front. Left side. Only once have I ever not sat in my seat.

That didn't work out so well.

We rode against the traffic. We were eastbound and everything was mostly clear, every once in a while a Volkswagen Cabriolet, Nissan Leopard or Maxima, or maybe a Volvo 780. I saw a Volkswagen Thing once. Westbound on the other hand was practically standstill. People driving to the factory. Their cars were composed of the palette of rusted-out American: Falcons, Rampages, Darts, Meteors, Lasers, and Hondas, which weren't American cars but were products of our town. The westbound cars had defensive bumper stickers: "Don't

Laugh It's Paid For"; "Don't Laugh At Least It Runs"; "Don't Laugh Your Daughter Might Be In Here."

The eastbound were all college people, like people of the college. Rutherford College in town—at one point last year the cover model of *Time* magazine's report on the absurd cost of private colleges—was the most expensive college in the US in 1984–85. After that report came out, applications to the college rose fifteen percent. The bumper stickers on the eastbound cars advertised better colleges: Dartmouth, Harvard, Oberlin, Middlebury.

The town was founded by limestone barons of the nineteenth century. It was originally called Mingo, which was what whites called the Mingwe, which was what the Eastern Algonquins called the Iroquois-speaking tribes that moved here in the eighteenth century. Then Rutherford B. Hayes was born here and became president in 1877 and it was renamed Rutherford in his honor, even though you'd think it should've been named Hayes.

Accuracy in naming things isn't necessarily a strong suit in this part of the country.

Sprinkled throughout the city were spent quarries, giant holes where the limestone had been torn from the earth and then donated back to the city for use as parkland and a tax write-off for the barons. The biggest one was at the center of the town. Blue Limestone was what everyone called it, even though it was gray and depressing. It was so deep no one is said to have touched the bottom and lived. It was the giant drain hole that our little lives circled. The high school kids had a legendary party there at the end of every school year with a bonfire so big you could see its glow from anywhere in town.

The town had two main industries: the factory and the college.

The factory was three shifts. It made Honda Accords, which are and are not American cars. The plant was, my dad claimed, more Public Relations than anything else, a way to keep people from freaking out about imports. He worked at the college. He was an adjunct, which means he was and was not a professor. My mom liked to say that everyone treated him like a professor except his colleagues and his paycheck. She said that Dad's problem was that he was overeducated and underutilized; she said he's got smarts that are going stagnant teaching eight sections of Intro to Modern Thought. I don't know how smart my dad is; I just know my mom was always telling me how smart he is.

My mom worked for Marriott. She did project analysis. She flew to places Marriott was thinking about building a Marriott and told them if it was a good place to build a Marriott. She was gone a lot. I got a postcard from her on Saturday from South Korea. It had a palace on it. She wished me luck, told me she was sad she wasn't home, told me she couldn't believe her baby was in high school, told me something else but it was covered up by the stamp cancellation. I knew that I should have known how long she'd be gone for but I'd forgotten. It was hard to keep track of her absences.

The bus driver started punching the horn. I looked up just as she hit the brakes and the metal bar of the seat in front of me popped me in the chin. The metal taste of blood filled my mouth. I peeked out the window at what was going on. A red Saab was tearing right at us in our lane. He was dragging honks from every car he whipped by. He was going fifty-five easy and skipping along outside of traffic in our lane.

We were at a full stop and I was bracing for impact even though he was two hundred yards away. As a rule I think it's never too early to start bracing for impact. I was staring at the seat back in front of me. It was upholstered in dark green vinyl, a green so dark it was almost black, a black so cold it was like a milkshake.

Right before he was about to plow right into us, traffic opened up and the Saab dipped back into his rightful lane, as if he had planned it that way the whole time. In the front seat of the Saab, the driver and passenger were brown-skinned and wearing what looked like turbans. The driver was talking to the passenger. Waving his hands in the air, he seemed unaware that he'd almost smashed into a school bus, unconcerned with the chaos he'd caused.

Saab. Turbans. Brown skin. Driving the wrong way in traffic. Any one of the four would get your ass beat in this town. A Saab wasn't just foreign, it was snooty foreign.

A Saab wasn't even a car you'd see in Columbus. More like a Cincinnati car. They put chili on pasta in Cincinnati. They were used to exotic things there.

The bus stopped at the lip of the trailer park. Seven kids got on. Holly Trowbridge, who was in my grade, was totally having sex. In seventh grade, she told the health teacher that douching with Coca-Cola prevented pregnancies. This was in front of the whole class.

I wanted to tell her about the Saab.

"Morning, Holly," I said to her.

"Don't talk to me, Yo-Yo Fag," she said.

Her two younger brothers laughed as she said it. Two more trailer park kids said Yo-Yo Fag as if it was an echo in the bus. It was my name. It'd been my name since sixth grade. I was Yo-Yo Fag. I was hoping that with the switch to high school I could also scuttle my nickname. But no. No one was going to forget a nickname like mine.

We rolled through downtown, picked up a couple more kids. Porky Boxwell gave me a dope slap as he passed by. He and Holly sat in the way back. Porky was basically all baby fat, mullet, and undeveloped chin. Holly found him irresistible.

One time when we were waiting for the bus after school, Porky had picked me up off the ground by putting two fingers in each of my armpits. I had bruises that no one ever saw. The worst part of it was the way I had laughed weakly as Porky held me aloft, like I wanted to act as if we were both working together as he hurt and humiliated me. Trying to force myself to laugh about it kept me from crying.

"What's up, Yo-Yo Fag?" Kurt Gummo shouted as he waddled in. Seventh grader. Five-two, 225.

"People should call you the Blob," I said.

"Eat me, gerbil penis."

"Language," the bus driver said, glaring at Kurt in her big rectangular rearview mirror.

This was Rutherford, Ohio, where "penis" was considered swearing but "fag" was acceptable. Being a fag was worse than calling someone a fag. I wasn't gay but I was called a fag because I had refused to share my yo-yo with Shane Colton in sixth grade.

"Fuck you then, you yo-yo fag," he had muttered. I thought no one had heard.

But the Colton family in our county was a breeding force equal to none. They were, in the words of SAT prep, both capricious and ubiquitous. My nickname spread throughout Hayes Intermediate by week's end. The name had stuck through middle school, and it seemed it was going to continue to stick through high school.

It was August 25, 1985, and I was the Yo-Yo Fag of Rutherford County, Ohio.

CHAPTER 2

MY HOMEROOM WAS REALLY not all that new. We were in the same building we were in for junior high, now we were just in the other half. Construction was being done on the new high school over on Euclid Avenue, some sprawling design from a California architect, a fact that had been a big part of the bond issue campaign, as if "California Architect" was a signifier of the highest possible quality.

The building we were in was constructed during the WPA. Well, half of it was—the other half was built during the fifties, an addition made with no attempt to join the two by any design concept. It was a massive building cleaved down the center—the junior high on the old side, the high school on the newer side, with just a single narrow hallway connecting the two. It was a new room but homerooms are assigned by last name and grade. I'd been standing in lines next to these kids forever.

Our teacher was Mrs. Black. She told us all to call her "Mzzz Black" but within ten minutes it was clear that it was not going to stick. Mrs. Black's husband was my dentist. He once took my mom, dad, and me out on his boat on Lake Erie to fish. My dad and he got to be buddies somehow or other. My dad ended up friends with a lot of these professional guys who like to have a philosopher friend. Made them feel smart or something. They adopted my dad like a weak kitten. They bought him lunch and told him their justifications for the shitty things they did. That was what they thought philosophy was: justifications for being an asshole.

You know who's awful? Dentists who read Nietzsche.

What my dad actually did was draw diagrams and equations and stare at them for an hour or so before giving up. He said it was the benchwork of philosophy that no one cared about. His dissertation was a diagramming of a sentence by Hegel in the original German and then in three different English translations. It was five hundred pages long. We used it to keep the living room window open in the summer.

Mrs. Black read roll. Maybe because I knew her outside of school, maybe because I'd mowed her lawn and helped clean her basement when it flooded this summer, maybe because I'd seen her in a swimsuit, maybe I just expected a little bit of kindness. But she read my full name anyway.

"Baruch Nadler?"

"Barry," I said while raising my hand. "I go by Barry."

I was not sure what I expected. It was going to be a long day of correcting teachers.

I was named after Baruch Spinoza, a seventeenth-century Jewish philosopher from Amsterdam. Hegel supposedly said, "You're either a Spinozist or not a philosopher at all." Which is why my dad bullied my mom into this ridiculous name. So, I have a Jewish first name which means "blessed" and gets me punched after class. Try being this kid with this name in this town—the kind of place where most people thought "Jewish" was a kind of salad dressing.

Maybe Yo-Yo Fag was a blessing.

The factory's kids run the schools. I was of different stock than they were. Thinner-boned, weaker-skinned, a more tender build, shortest kid in my class eight years running. I barely survived the moments in between classes. I paid attention in class because I wanted that time to extend and last forever. Wrap me in the triple-fold of fatted sacrifice Odysseus offers up to Algebra Two; let me remain physics-drenched and band-tired. My greatest wish was for there to be human-sized pneumatic tubes I could climb in and be sucked through from class to class.

Just don't put me in the hallways where the real owners of this town reinforce their lien on my body. Fag tags, red necks, Indian burns, knuckle punches, charley horses, calf bites, wedgies, purple nurples, swirlies, frogging, dope slaps, sternum typewriters, two hits for flinching, "stop hitting yourself, stop hitting yourself." It's one thing to be weak in this world, it's another to be reminded of it all the time.

By assholes.

"Welcome, students." The speaker over the door crackled and came to life. "Let's start the day with the pledge of allegiance."

And the day went on from there.

Every class I got called Baruch. Every class I corrected the teacher while the other kids giggled. "I go by Barry," I said at least eight times.

CHAPTER 3

THE BUS RIDE HOME was the bus ride home.

Three rows from the front and to the left.

Yo-Yo Fags all around. The smell of first-day cologne and perfume was replaced by the stink of hormones; of pheromones; of erections and menstruations that no one knew how to properly deal with. We were all acolytes in these bodies. Trainees without the manual or appropriate supervision.

We pulled to a stop at the railroad crossing. The bus driver opened the door to check for trains. A guy with jean shorts, combat boots, and no shirt crossed the tracks. His Doberman, who wasn't on a leash, trotted behind him. The dog stopped at the tracks, pawing at the rocks of the crossing. The guy turned and whistled. The dog lay down and whined. We were all watching and he knew it. He whistled again, two fingers in his mouth: high, piercing. He was probably famous in his family for that whistle.

The dog did not move. The train tracks were freaking it out. The guy was maybe twenty and skinny with muscle, like all he ever ate was beef jerky. He stomped his foot at the dog but it still didn't move. He slapped it on the head. He slapped it on its butt. The dog still didn't move, just took the hits. He closed his fists and started punching the dog. We heard the thud of the punches and the jangle of the dog's choke chain. He hit the dog in the jaw, in the chest, kicked it in the stomach. The dog didn't fight back. It was a Doberman pinscher. It could've torn this guy's neck out. It took the beating. Whining and yelping at the blows.

We were all church-silent watching this. It was too early in the school year for any of us to process this.

The bus driver jammed the emergency brake down. She was outside before any of us knew it. She had the paddle with her and she was yelling at the man. The man yelled back.

I heard, "God's creature." I heard, "My dog." I heard, "Police and don't think I won't."

The man spat hard on the ground like it was the grammatical hard stop to their fight. He then picked the dog up and tossed it over his shoulder. The dog's claws left pink lines on his redneck flesh.

"Holy sweater," said the Blob.

The man strutted down the street with the dog over his shoulder. The dog licked his ear. I felt nauseous. After all of that man punching the hell out of the dog, it was the dog licking the man's ear that made me want to puke.

This was the end of my first day of high school.

CHAPTER 4

AT HOME, THERE WAS A NOTE from Dad to not disturb him and a bouquet of cookies on sticks from Cheryl's Cookies from my mom. College started in two weeks, and I wasn't going to see my dad a whole lot until then. He always forgot to plan his classes until the last minute and he never kept hard copies of his previous syllabuses. He said it kept him fresh. He was always worried about falling into a rut. If mom was here she'd tell him that worrying about falling into a rut was its own kind of rut.

I plucked three cookies, got a pack of matches, and went outside to burn stuff.

CHAPTER 5

THE NEXT DAY, the bus was six minutes late. People honked as they drove by. Some dude flipped me off. I flinched every time a car went by. I'm the free pass for other people's casual aggression. I have on my jeans and a different Batman t-shirt on. My mom wants me to dress like my peers. She says it like that. My peers. She wants me to be popular with my peers and she thinks that you dress for the friends you aspire to have. I want to own enough Batman t-shirts to have a different one for each day of the week.

The bus stopped in front of me and the doors collapsed open. I mumbled good morning to the driver. I don't mention anything about her being late. She probably had a complicated life.

I was the first person the bus picked up so what I was seeing was impossible. I was the farthest kid out. But three rows from the front and to the left was a brown kid in a turban. He was in my seat. Not knowing what to do, and fearing being caught in any other seat, I sat down next to him. We were two guys on an empty bus sitting next to each other. The gears ground into place.

"Gurbaksh," he said and offered his hand to me.

"Barry," I said.

"You must be a very friendly person," he said. "I hate first days of school."

"This is the second day," I said.

"Do you chew tobacco?" he asked.

"I'm sorry?"

"I have this idea in my head that every boy in Ohio chews tobacco."

"What about the girls?"

"Only girls in private schools chew tobacco. I hear it's because it's an appetite suppressant. They also cut themselves but that's not an appetite suppressant, that's externalized self-hatred."

He didn't speak like I expected a guy in a turban to speak. Instead he had almost a Minnesotan accent. Mostly weird exaggerated *o*'s.

"You've been in a lot of private schools?" I asked.

"Mostly." He tilted his head a little. "This is only my third public school."

"It's my only school, period."

"My dad moves around for business a lot. As well as for personal stuff."

"What else are girls in private school like?"

"It depends if it's a boarding one or not. Boarding schools, everyone is kind of shitty. It's like what a kennel would be like if you stopped feeding the dogs. You learn fast that girls are dogs like everyone else."

"What's with the turban?"

"I'm a Sikh, man."

"Like the Golden Temple?"

He looked at me sideways. "What do you know about the Golden Temple?"

"My mom sent me a postcard from Amritsar once," I said. And because he kept looking at me, I added, "She works for Marriott. She was in talks to build a hotel there but India's too protectionist and wanted too much control." I blushed. I hated it when I ran at the mouth.

There was silence. The slight hiccup of the engine noise as the bus lady changed gears. The cars toddling past us. A terrifyingly thin, absurdly made-up woman walked on the broken sidewalks under the train bridge. Lipstick and stretch pants, swinging her arms vigorous-like. It was seven in the morning. Gurbaksh was nodding like he was doing silent computations in his head.

It was too weird to be sitting together on an empty bus and not talking. "Are you from Amritsar?"

"Toronto," he said. "You're the first white person I've met who has ever known anything about being a Sikh."

"If it makes you feel any better, I don't know anything about Toronto."

"You know what a Sikh is and don't know anything about Canada?"

"I have a library card," I said. I only knew about the Golden Temple from the postcard and I was afraid he'd ask more detailed questions about what I knew of Sikhism so I changed the topic. "What does your dad do that keeps you all moving so much?"

"He's a liar," he replied.

"A lawyer?"

"No. A liar. He's kind of an engineer without, you know, any degrees to back it up with." Gurbaksh shifted in his seat. "He stays at a place until they decide to check his references. Then we move."

"Whoa."

"Yeah. Every place we move to, the students at the school usually think I'm a foreign exchange student. I've started thinking about my dad as my host family. It's easier to deal with that way. He's just someone I'm staying with for a discrete amount of time."

There was a loud commotion as the bus ground to a halt. Porky Boxwell and Holly Trowbridge were screaming at each other. She had a fistful of his hair as he tried to climb the steps. She was bigger than him by four inches and fifteen pounds but most of her punches landed on his backpack. They collapsed on the bus floor and Porky curled into a ball. The bus driver was trying to pull Holly off of him.

She got her off and Holly kicked at Porky as he escaped to the back of the bus. The bus driver made Holly sit in the front, right next to the redheaded girl who somehow got on during all of this. She was some kind of ninja. Holly started crying.

"They must be boyfriend/girlfriend," Gurbaksh said.

I told him about the health class and Holly and the Coca-Cola.

"Oh lord. So they'll breed," Gurbaksh said. "The stupid ones get laid all the time."

After the Blob got on, Gurbaksh turned to me. "Why did he call you Yo-Yo Fag?"

I shook my head.

Gurbaksh started laughing. "That's the funniest nickname I've ever heard."

"I try not to hear it."

Gurbaksh shrugged his shoulders. "That shit is at least original. I can't wait to hear what they'll call me."

In the back of the bus Porky and Holly were continuing their argument separated by five rows of seats.

"Yo-Yo Fag," Gurbaksh said. "This is the first time I've been optimistic about this place."

When we got to school, Gurbaksh waved to me as he disappeared through the doors. "See ya, Yo-Yo Fag."

CHAPTER 6

THE FIRST CLASS OF THE DAY was English. It was taught by a frazzled chubby little mouse of a guy named Mr. Morris. He wore a bright orange polo the first day. We had to let him know that the size sticker was still on the shirt. Once he'd peeled the sticker off I noticed that the shirt still had the creases from the way it had been folded at the store. Today he was wearing what must be his regular clothes. A crap button-down and a thin old cardigan that was shiny at the elbows.

Teachers always try to sell you on the subject the first couple of days. The halls were as thick with evangelism as they were with hair spray applied by amateurs. Mr. Morris at least didn't try to convince us of the importance of English. Maybe he was burnt out.

We were supposed to write about something that struck us as having sublimity. We read a poem about a mountain. He defined the sublime five different ways. I was so confused about what we were supposed to write that I wrote about the guy I saw beating his dog in the middle of the street.

Honors Science was kind of cool. The teacher was a kind of celebrity in town. Reagan wanted to send a teacher into space. Mr. Reynolds was one of fifty thousand NASA applicants and he made it past a couple of cuts before being rejected. He wore his pin and his hat. He told us that space was the future, that within our lifetimes we'd have a space community and we'd all become real citizens of the cosmos. It was cool. You think about living in zero gravity and your brain has this little hitch where it can't really conceive of it. All the movies about space, ships always have their own gravity. Everybody isn't always just floating around all the time, which is too bad because that would be the best part of space.

Science is cooler than philosophy because they're developing new ways of living. New ways of being. Philosophy is stuck on trying to describe who we are and why we are. I'm going to tell my dad I'm going to be a scientist.

CHAPTER 7

On my locker someone had drawn this in thick marker:

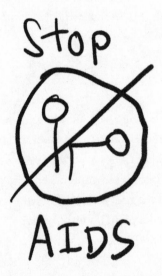

The custodian gave me a bucket, a sponge, gloves, and some spray he told me not to get anywhere near my skin. I missed PE that day scrubbing it off.

CHAPTER 8

IT WAS IN SEVENTH PERIOD when the speaker came on. It was during band. I was third chair trumpet. There were four of us. I sat next to Flossie Beckley, a girl so heartbreakingly beautiful that I'd gladly collect and ferment the leavings of her spit valve and drink down the resultant wine. We were sight-reading a Sousa piece when the voice came on.

"Mr. Kendrix?"

We kept playing.

"Mr. Kendrix?" the voice said louder. Some of the kids stopped playing but Kendrix kept conducting, shooting all of us evil looks, daring us to stop without his say-so. He was a very thin tall man who had talked me into the trumpet when I was in fourth grade, saying it was what all the cool guys played. He'd gotten grayer since then but hadn't gained a pound. Inexplicably he had a little bit of a wattle under his neck and it swayed as he popped his baton up down right left. He was having a power struggle with the voice on the speaker. He and only he stopped the music. Most of us had trailed away, only a couple of the flutes and Roxanne Nolan on the clarinet kept going.

Roxanne was an ass-kisser. She stared at Mr. Kendrix as if he should know she was his only true disciple. It was never a question for Roxanne Nolan that only Mr. Kendrix stopped the music. There could be nuclear attacks, swarms of locusts, Russian soldiers storming into the room, and Roxanne would keep playing until Mr. Kendrix did that little sky-cursive motion with his baton and clasped his other hand into a fist.

"Mr. Kendrix," the voice was now near screaming.

Kendrix chewed his bottom lip, swung his hands in the "all silent" move, and then pushed his hands down so we could all lower our instruments. He put his hands on the lectern and exhaled dramatically a couple of times before he shouted, "Yes?"

"Baruch Nadler needs to come to the office."

I liked getting called to the office. It was like I was a little bit famous. I put my trumpet away in its velvet-lined box and put it in my band cubby.

I shouldered my backpack and made my way through the halls. The two halves of the building were connected by a corpus callosum of a marble staircase whose pitch was ten to fifteen degrees steeper than code. It was always a delicate act getting down the steps, the front edges of which had been smoothed down and made slippery by decades of school shoes. Going down alone was difficult enough. The steps were the choke point between the halves of the building and so going down between classes with the herd of hormone-cases was an invitation to a concussion.

"I'm here," I said to the office lady. "The office called for me to come down."

The room was all yellowish wood that shined from the years of use. The sun slanted through the blinds and made the glass on top of the counter separating the waiting area from the offices in back almost too bright.

The office lady had hair that was like a pile of spun sugar dyed an unnatural blond. She was so skinny her dresses always hung off of her like robes. She looked like a Q-tip with a lot of foundation.

"What's your name, dear?"

Behind me there sat three big kids. Big kids shifting in wooden chairs. Why'd she have to call me dear?

"Barry Nadler."

"Barry?"

"It might say Baruch," I said.

"There you are. I'll let Mrs. Gildea know you're here."

I sat in the only free chair. The guys next to me both had their arms on the armrests. I couldn't put my arms up there without accidentally touching their elbows. When you're Yo-Yo Fag, you've got to watch stuff like that.

Don't touch guys.

Even accidentally.

The guy next to me was Randy Colton. There was no one more famous than Randy Colton. Randy Colton flunked sixth grade two times. It was my class that he finally started passing. He was six feet tall and built like a man. He was wearing a green army jacket that stunk of cigarettes. His dad had been in Vietnam. In seventh-grade history he gave a presentation on the Mai Lai massacre and failed because he kept calling the Vietnamese "gooks." My dad was not in Vietnam. He'd gotten a student deferment. Randy Colton's dad had killed people. My dad diagrammed sentences.

I had been in gym classes with Randy every year since sixth grade. It was its own kind of hell. In gym class, we play a game that's a variation of dodgeball. It's called Kill Ball. It's played not with an oversized kickball ball but with volleyballs, four of them. The rules of Kill Ball are absurdly simple. You aren't out when you're hit with a ball, you're out when you can't take it anymore.

The gym teacher Mr. Harolds developed the game in response to the ban on paddling students. He sat in the bleachers chewing gum and watched us peg one another as hard as we could with the volleyballs. The fact that there were four volleyballs meant you could never really keep yourself safe. In dodgeball, you watch the big red ball and avoid it. In Kill Ball, you watch one ball, you get pegged with two others. Randy Colton was a prodigy at the game.

It was Achilles against a kindergarten class.

I saw him peg Brent Gates so hard that he flipped over and landed on his neck. Mr. Harolds was interested in creating men. To Mr. Harolds men were created within a cocoon of bruises and concussions.

I knew how Darwinism worked, so I'd call myself out at the beginning of the game and run laps on the track that circled the gym.

Randy Colton was in the office because he was in trouble. The second day and he was in trouble. It's nice having your burnouts be so reliable.

Mrs. Gildea was a guidance counselor. Guidance counselors' offices were the safest spaces for kids like me, even better than the classrooms. They were caverns to which we could retire, furnished with scrying pools where our fabulous fortunes were foretold. When you test well, the future is always better than the now. And I reliably tested in the ninety-eighth percentile.

That's in the country. My scores showed that I was better than this school. Only in the guidance counselor's office was I given the respect I was due. Let the glue-sniffers get scolded by the vice-principal, I had the rest of my life to plot out.

"Hey, man," Randy said to me. "Do you know what AIDS stands for?"

"It's Acquired Immunodeficiency Syndrome," I said.

Randy shook his head. "No, man. It's Anally Injected Death Syndrome." And he laughed so hard that the woman behind the desk gave him a look that would have frozen most land mammals.

Mrs. Gildea came out.

"Baruch Nadler," she said.

"The fuck kind of name is that?" Randy Colton asked.

I followed her back into her office.

Mrs. Gildea had gotten some new posters. One was Kermit the Frog with a book that was about how important reading was. There was a framed picture of Larry Bird, one of Jane Pauley, and one of Julia Child. They were all signed. There was one of Bill Cosby too. His wasn't signed.

"Baruch," Mrs. Gildea said and motioned to the chair. Her office was small and had no windows.

"I go by Barry."

"That's right, you do," she said, after glancing at a file. "How have you been?"

I expected a hug or a handshake or one of those side hugs teachers start giving you when they don't have to squat down to your level anymore but they don't want to come into contact with your genitals.

"Fine," I said.

Mrs. Gildea sat there for a moment with her mouth open. She looked a little like a cocker spaniel, her hair flopping over her ears and her little nose, her glasses making her eyes kind of bugged out.

"Summer was fine, I guess," I added. "I read a lot. I read about slavery like all summer."

She didn't make a note of that in her file. That seemed like college app gold: reading and history? I hoped she was good at her job.

She tented her fingers. "Barry, I like to take some time in the beginning of the year to meet with students who, well, live in unorthodox situations—broken homes and such."

"My home isn't broken," I said.

"But your mother travels a lot, doesn't she?"

"Yes, she sends me a lot of postcards. We don't talk on the phone because of the long-distance charges. But we keep up a lively correspondence."

"She's gone a lot, isn't she?"

"Probably three out of four weeks."

"And your father? He works for the university still?"

"Yes," I answered. "He mostly teaches the Intro classes so it's kind of like I'm already going to college by living with him."

"He teaches you then? You talk? Every night? Every day? Do you have dinners, just meals, together?"

"No. I cook for myself. His work is very exacting," I said. My palms weren't sweating anymore. I was back in control. "I read the books he leaves around. *Lives of the Philosophers*. That kind of stuff."

"And that's as interesting to you as slavery?"

"Well, it's like examples of ways of being smart. Baruch Spinoza, my namesake, was talking with two friends about his views on God and the Torah. They knew a little bit how he felt and they kind of like goaded him into harsher ways of articulating his views. These two friends then went and told the Elders about Spinoza's views and he was excommunicated." I waited for her to be impressed. She should be impressed. "Like the best philosopher since Aristotle was caught by a couple dummies who just asked him what he really felt. You can be smart and really dumb at the same time."

"Is it dumb to say what you really feel?" she asked.

"No," I said, remembering that I was in a guidance counselor's office. "But the things we feel . . . there's also like intellect. Intellect is there to protect the feelings from dummies who'll betray you. My dad taught me this. He's taught me discipline."

"Discipline?" Her ears perked up. Mrs. Gildea wrote something in her notebook and then leaned forward as if she was going to confide in me. She didn't write down anything else I'd said until I'd stumbled onto one of her button words. "That brings me to one of the things I wanted to talk to you about. You missed PE yesterday." She let a quantum of quiet radiate for a moment. "Each class you miss earns you a detention, you know."

I swallowed hard. "Someone had drawn on my locker." I felt so stupid, caught by such an obvious trap. "I was scrubbing it off."

"What was it?" She was still leaning forward.

My breathing took a funny turn, like it got confused if it was supposed to inhale or exhale and the air got caught in my throat until it was all figured out.

"Nothing." I tore the Kleenex into little strips and wound the little strips around my fingers and then flexed my fingers and burst the strips.

"Are you engaging in," she paused trying to find the words, "risky behaviors?"

"What? No."

"Are you having urges?" She cleared her throat. "Perhaps of the, well, untraditional variety?"

I stared at her agape. My head was going full-tilt shitstorm carnival ride. All I had for her was silence.

"I just want to let you know—I'm not sure you've been reading the news—but there's a terrible disease going around in some, well, untraditional communities. And, um, I just want you to know you can talk to me, talk to any of the counseling staff, before you, um, engage in those untraditional, well, practices."

My brain was going nuts, but I thought she might've been asking if I was gay. Like because somebody had written it on my locker it made it true. This was absolutely the worst way to be called a faggot—some awful $10,000 Pyramid method of just saying clue-words and not the thing itself. I wanted to jump at her, claw her glasses right off her stupid cocker spaniel face.

After a few portentous moments during which she gave me her full condescending "you can talk to me" moist eyeballs, Mrs. Gildea leaned back. "Your English teacher, Mr. Morris, has shared with me an essay of yours."

She pulled out a piece of paper. It was a mimeographed copy of the essay I'd written in class the other day. I knew what essay it was. We'd only written one. "There's some pretty violent stuff in there. A man beating a dog and then the dog licking the man's neck? Why does the dog lick the man's neck do you think?"

"It's just what happened. It was on the bus ride to school yesterday." Was I being accused of something here? I thought it was a good essay. "You can ask anyone on the bus. The bus lady went out and challenged the guy. She'll tell you it really happened."

"It's not about what happened or not," Mrs. Gildea said. "It's that you chose to write about it. That's what concerns me."

"But it happened. So I wrote about it."

"You seem, in this essay, to be really concerned for the dog."

"He was punching her."

"So why does the dog lick the man's neck?"

"You'd have to ask her," I said, and because I couldn't stop myself I added, "Do you speak dog?"

Mrs. Gildea spun sideways in her chair away from me. "This doesn't need to be confrontational, Barry."

"What *does* it need to be?" I felt my throat get tight and my voice was squeaking a little. But this was not going all right. This was unfair. My chest was collapsing on itself. What was going on with my chest? "This is bullshit," I said and regretted it immediately.

Mrs. Gildea folded her notebook and capped her pen. She gave me a look. I'd crossed a line. My lungs were trying to switch places with each other in my chest. My head was a confetti parade.

My brain was rushing so fast the rest of the world had become syrup. The room was full of data and it was all trying to bum-rush my head. The tags on the folders, the words on the files. My brain was too full and more was clamoring to get in (the paint-loaded molding, the freckles on the drop ceiling, Mrs. Gildea had a gold tooth!—left side, right before her molar). I stood up and my chair banged off the back wall. Glass broke. Larry Bird fell to the floor.

"You tell people to write whatever they want but it works like the Stasi here." I knew I was in trouble but I kept going. Once you break a school employee's stuff and tell her that she's the Stasi you might as well go full feral.

I grabbed the filing cabinet but it was too heavy, so I shook it hard until I exhausted myself. All the files on top of the cabinet slid off and splayed open on the floor. I put my back against the file cabinet and slid down the gray metal of the thing and sat on the floor. There was broken glass, papers. I still couldn't breathe. I wanted to puke but my stomach and mouth didn't seem to be connected anymore.

The door to her office slammed open. The principal, the vice-principal, and Randy Colton all stood there.

I wished I could make myself pass out. Make them have to carry me wherever they wanted me to go. I was done being the one who had to move my body where they wanted it to go.

Randy hooted and clapped as I was led from the office to the nurse's.

CHAPTER 9

THE CAR RIDE HOME was silent. I went to my room when we got home. So did my father. At 11:00 p.m., I took a bath and read a book by Harriet Jacobs, who escaped slavery and then lived in an attic where she couldn't sit or stand up but she could watch her children through peepholes in the wood. I thought of my mom and immediately was ashamed for comparing my mom living in hotel rooms and peeping at me through postcards to what Harriet Jacobs went through. Sometimes reading is about helping to connect yourself to your own emotions; most of the time, though, it was about how small and little your life was in comparison to what other people lived through.

I ate a sleeve of graham crackers, then went to bed.

On my pillow was a note from my dad. The school called. I'd been suspended for three days. I was supposed to seek counseling and present evidence of that search before I was to come back. Dad wrote that he'd get someone at the university to sign off on the forms without me needing to meet with anyone. I'd had two days of high school and now I was suspended for three. Some kind of record.

CHAPTER 10

THE NEXT DAY, I woke up late. Dad took me to breakfast at the restaurant in the grocery store across the street. He was a regular. He had a booth that was his, according to the waitress who sat us.

"I know you want coffee," she said to my father. "What are you gonna want to drink this morning, Mister Man?"

"I'll have coffee too." I looked at my dad to see if he'd object. He didn't. I wished he would've. I'd much rather have had a Dr Pepper.

The waitress left a menu for me but not for Dad. His footprint was large at the restaurant in the grocery store. My dad had brought the newspaper. It sat folded up on the table. Both of us tried to act like we didn't want to be reading it.

Our coffees came, along with a cold little dish containing a pyramid of creamers. My dad grabbed one but didn't put it in his coffee. I took one as well. The little pyramid collapsed. I poured my creamer into my coffee. It made a swirl of clouds in the blackness. I stared at the clouds and grabbed another creamer and poured it in. It was a game between my father and me. Who would talk first? I could maybe make it through the breakfast by just watching the khaki clouds settle in my cup.

The waitress came back. "What's the meaning of life today, Professor?"

"Today it's two eggs over medium, bacon extra crisp, and whole wheat toast." Dad looked at me. "What do you want?"

"Pancakes," I said. "And bacon."

"You want that short or tall stack?"

I didn't know what she was saying. Did they stack the bacon? Like part of the curing process? Was short like raw? I didn't want raw bacon. Who would serve raw bacon? Isn't that a recipe for trichinosis? The tension began in my chest. It started pushing the air out of me. I couldn't order breakfast. That's how dumb I was.

"He'll have the tall stack," my dad said, rescuing me. "He's a growing boy."

"It comes with eggs. How do you want them?"

Jesus Christ, how many questions were there?

"Maybe fried," I said. "But not so that they're gooey in the middle?" The thought of yolks bursting and creeping down my plate suddenly made me nauseous.

"Over medium," my dad said.

"And toast: white, rye, whole wheat, or biscuit?"

I hated her.

"He'll take a biscuit."

"Good choice. They're real fresh today. I'll throw in one for you too, Professor." The waitress took the menu and gave my dad a wink.

"How's the softball team, Stacey?" my dad asked.

"We're good," she replied. "Better than we have any right to be, at least."

"Your humility is your strong suit," my dad said. It was amazing watching him talk with her. He did it so easily. More easily than he ever did with me. It was like spending all day walking on the street with a frog and then getting to a pond and seeing it swim for the first time. All that awkward architecture of its body being put to perfect use. How did this recluse at home have charisma for a waitress?

"You need refills on coffee, you just wave me down, okay?"

My dad looked at the paper. Something that happened yesterday in the world caught his attention and he pulled the paper next to his coffee.

After a few minutes of reading, he asked, "Who is the second person Raskolnikov kills in *Crime and Punishment*?"

"Lizaveta, the pawnbroker's half sister."

"You're fourteen." My dad pulled at his collar and adjusted his glasses. "You should not know that by heart."

"I'm precocious," I said.

"I'm going to start paying more attention to what you're reading. I think you're getting too maudlin too fast."

I nodded as if this were a welcome thing, knowing he'd never follow through on it.

My pancakes came. They were revolting. As I ate them all I could do was imagine vomiting them up later. The smell of maple syrup and butter mixed with stomach acids. How could you not remember Lizaveta? I tore my biscuit and stabbed it into the egg yolk because it seemed like the most disgusting thing to do.

"When is Mom coming home?" I asked.

My dad took off his glasses. I tried to read the state of their marriage in the way he rubbed his eyes before he answered my question. "Her project has been held up. She'll be another two weeks at least."

"She's still in Seoul?"

"Morocco." My dad put his glasses back on and unfolded the paper. He handed me the Arts section. "She got called to Morocco. Should be home in two weeks if all goes well."

Dad and I read the paper for the rest of breakfast. I read the comics. I tried as hard as I could to be amused by drunk Andy Capp beating his wife or by the obese cat or by Beetle Bailey, the soldier who wanted nothing to do with being in the army but was stuck in it no matter how much he disobeyed.

This reading was so much more inappropriate than Dostoyevsky.

CHAPTER 11

I WAS OUTSIDE in our driveway. I'd bought a case of Scot-Lad soda, an off-brand array of knockoffs of popular sodas at pennies a can. I was tossing them up and hitting them with a bat. They smashed whether or not I made contact, spraying sugar-water everywhere when they landed on the asphalt. It was a big goddamn day for the ants.

"Yo-Yo Fag!"

I flinched.

There was a squeal of brakes and someone yelling that name again. Gurbaksh yelled right by my ear, "You naughty naughty boy."

"You heard?" I asked.

"Randy Colton saw the whole thing and told everybody."

"I'm fucked, Gurbaksh."

"It's Gary," he said. "They call me Gary here."

"Of course they do."

"It's either that or listen to the toothless yokels mangle my name. Like how we call Deutschland 'Germany.'"

"I've never understood that." I pitched another Scot-Lad to myself and missed it. It landed and spun at my feet. "Like shouldn't we just call things by the names the people who live there call them? Is it really so hard?"

"I've looked this up because I get renamed so many times. The word is exonym for the things other people call it and an endonym for what the people themselves call it."

"Damn. It's fucked up that there's words for that."

Gurbaksh shrugged a what-are-you-gonna-do shrug then he smiled wide. "Yes. Gary and Yo-Yo Fag," he announced and then whispered, "their real names altered to protect the stupids."

"Gary and Barry sounds better," I said. Gurbaksh didn't hear me. He picked up one of the sodas and opened it. He took a swig, made a face, and then set it back down. "So does everyone think I'm crazy?"

"Yes," he shouted. "Like crazy badass, like crazy unpredictable, like crazy cool. People want us to come to their parties. Like junior and senior parties. People are a little afraid of you."

"That's stupid," I said.

"That's high school. Meggie Morrison asked me if we were coming to her party on Saturday."

"Is she the one who looks like a turtle?" I could just picture her in my mind. Frosted lip gloss. Curly hair. Ghostly eyes. Sweaters.

"A sexy turtle," Gary crowed. "A turtle who let me feel her up after school yesterday."

"You've been busy."

"I'm living off your legend." Gary put his arm around my neck and kissed my cheek. "I'm the remoras to your shark."

"I think I'm grounded for a while."

"That reminds me, can we come over to dinner sometime? My dad wants to meet your dad."

"Why?"

"Who knows? Some old Punjabi nonsense. I told him about you and your mom and your dad and he got all excited to meet you all."

"My dad's kind of weird is all."

Gary put his hands on either side of his turban and adjusted it. "And my dad's a lunatic. It'll be fun. Is there good pizza in this town?"

"DelCo."

"The beer drive-thru?"

"They make good pizza," I said. "Greasy, but good." This is a fact of Rutherford, Ohio's cuisine: it's actually so bad it's amazing. When you strip yourself of judgement and expectations, lose the platonic ideal of "Pizza" haunting your brain, DelCo pizza is a revelation. Pair it with a Scot-Lad soda, and you'd have a kind of feast that activated vestigial taste buds, ones ghettoized by civilization and progress and sanitation, and the pure pleasure of the non-food would overwhelm you. It's the same kind of pleasure that comes in County Fair food—Dumbo ears, chili corn dogs, cotton candy, oversized pretzels slick with oil and covered in hail-sized chunks of salt, nachos in flimsy plastic trays with compartments overflowing with too-yellow cheese sauce and chili, flavored ice with syrup so violent it'd stain your shirt for good.

"Can we say Thursday?" Gary asked.

"It's that urgent?"

"My dad likes to know my best friend's parents." Gary smiled and imitated an Indian accent. "He wants to make sure I am surrounded with the best of influences."

"Sure," I said, stunned that I had a best friend.

Gary started talking about all the other parties we'd been invited to and the girls who'd been asking about me and the ones he wanted to feel up next. Feeling up seemed to be Gary's peak sexual experience.

"I'll have to ask my dad," I said.

Gary nodded. "It'll be cool. We'll bring everything. Seven o'clock. But my dad's always late so seven thirty. Your mom's not around is she?"

I shook my head. "Morocco."

"Just the boys then." Gary put his arm around me and hugged me close. "Oh, Yo-Yo Fag, this is going to be great."

CHAPTER 12

OUT OF TYPE, my dad said okay to Gurbaksh and his dad coming over. On my second day of suspension, I listened to the classic rock radio station until my head ached. I hated classic rock but I figured it would be part of my punishment, a Deep Purple penitence. I showered then rode my bike to the library. I tried to track down something on Sikhism. They didn't have a book just on Sikhism (they had to interlibrary loan that for me). They did have an Encyclopedia of World Religions I could look at but not check out. There were four paragraphs on Sikhism and an inset picture of the Golden Temple.

It was incredible. Even better than the postcard my mom had sent. The sun flickered off the filigreed bits. It was gold folded onto gold onto gold. And it was all sitting on a pond. The sun caught the pond and parts of the pond were gold too. It was like the building was so beautiful that it levitated. There were people walking around the temple, people in the water. A religion of gold, of beauty, of swimming. I tried to memorize the five paragraphs, the new words clapped away in my head: words I had no idea how to pronounce, words that kept falling to pieces in my head.

I carefully tore the picture out of the book. I wadded it up and put it in my mouth. It was thick, expensive paper. I didn't want to chew it. I slid the encyclopedia back on the shelf. I got outside, unlocked my bike, and the Golden Temple disintegrated in my mouth as I rode home.

CHAPTER 13

THE PIZZA ARRIVED before the Singhs did. Dad glared at me as he opened his wallet and shoved bills at the delivery boy.

"The house is a mess," he said and slammed the door. "Go do what you can to make it presentable."

"It's fine. They're bachelors too."

Dad gave me a look that let me know the cleaning up was more about punishment then presentation.

I pulled the laundry I'd been folding off of the couch, trying to keep the stacks of Dad's stuff and mine tidy in the basket while I heaved everything else on top. I'm the laundry guy in the house. I was twelve when I was elected to that position by a vote of two to one. Folding your parents' underwear is a hell of a way to go through puberty. You run the Oedipal gamut in a medium-sized load: the guilty erections handling Mom's delicates, the histrionic repulsion at Dad's skid marks. Adolescence is not for amateurs.

I had such limited access to pornography that the women's and teen's underwear sections of the Sears catalog qualified. I didn't keep them under my mattress. Movies had told me that was a cliché. And clichés were where moms will snoop. For Christmas when I was eleven I was given a miniature briefcase with a plastic infrastructure to hold and categorize cassette tapes. My mom had told someone that I was into music. My mom bought me the music she thought the popular kids in my school listened to: the Human League, Phil Collins, Bruce fucking Springsteen. The case was cheap and probably not even new when it was wrapped and sent to me. It was covered in light brown plastic leather and not even good plastic leather. I used a serrated kitchen knife and sawed the plastic inner casing out and put the best pages from the catalogs and magazines in there. It was my little box of sin. I felt like a perv whenever I opened it. Sometimes there'd be naked women in the movies Dad took me to and I'd hide my boner in the elastic of my pants until I'd get home and then rush to the closet, pull out my briefcase and jerk off. The briefcase made it professional-like, a final transaction to finish out the day.

To wake up to. To come home from school to do. To stop mowing the lawn to do.

I never masturbated twice in a row. I wanted to save that for my first time. This is how I dealt with feeling I was addicted to jerking off—I made rules.

1) No *National Geographic*s (I'm not sure if this was a rule or just a reaction. I'd always heard about *Nat Geo* being the place to find pix of naked women, but the only time I actually found a naked woman—after months of scouring through picture spreads on Iceland's glaciers, emperor penguins, the white squirrels of western North Carolina, the architecture of African anthills, and pages and pages of lava flowing—she was in a spread about a famine in Ethiopia. I jerked off to her emaciated nakedness in the library's bathroom—single occupancy, sturdy lock—and felt so awful that I didn't masturbate for two weeks.)

2) No masturbating on holidays. I did it once on Christmas and felt so guilty that I overcompensated in my thank-you notes.

Dearest Aunt Becky, Thank you from the bottom of my heart for the ten dollar check you sent to me. It's a gift that I will treasure and will make sure to put in a savings account so that I can spend it wisely later on in my future.

3) No redheads. I don't know why. They just gross me out. All doughy and freckles.

I hugged the laundry and humped it upstairs, then cleared the living room of old plates and glasses, scrubbed and flushed the toilet, and put the classical music station on the hi-fi. I was elbow-deep in dishwater when Mr. Singh knocked on the door. This is the first truth of hosting people: you make your house look like you don't live in it.

Mr. Singh opened the door before either Dad or I could get to it.

"Knock knock," he shouted into the house. "We have arrived."

His voice was deep. That was my first impression. Way deeper than any man I'd ever heard before. Like Darth Vader deep.

I toweled off my hands, ducked into the living room, and there was Dad shaking the hand of a man who was over six feet tall and that was before his turban. He was a solid guy, with a barrel chest and a potbelly, wearing a navy polo shirt tucked into his khakis. He was wearing penny loafers without socks. His salt-and-pepper beard was neatly trimmed and his nose was sharp. He was impeccably put together. My dad on the other hand was five-nine in an untucked flannel shirt, sweatpants, and gym socks. Unshaved. My dad was incapable of growing a beard, a talent he promised would be mine as well, so when he didn't shave, little patches of peach-fuzz stubble grew in random places. It was just one of the parts of his face that refused to become an adult. He still had acne every once in a while for God's sake.

After all the pleasantries were passed around, after I shook Mr. Singh's large hand and pulled away nearly crippled from his grasp, Mr. Singh snapped his fingers at Gary and he handed over two plastic bags drooping from his left hand to Mr. Singh, who presented them to my father. In them were two two-liters of Coke and Sprite and a six-pack of Budweiser.

"And your wife? Where is she this evening?" Mr. Singh asked.

"Out of the country, unfortunately."

"Some sort of vacation she's taking?"

"Work," my dad said and fluttered both of his hands in front of him to show how useless it was to keep track of a woman like his wife. "She's a motel scout. Identifies and develops properties."

"She sounds fascinating," Mr. Singh stated. "Does she use your last name? On these business trips?"

Gurbaksh buried his head in his hands.

My dad was bewildered and blinked away his confusion. "No. She uses her maiden name. We're both what you would call feminists, I guess."

My dad shrugged his shoulders. Again a gesture in the "who could tell with a woman like that" phylum.

"And she works for Marriott, you say?"

"I didn't but yes. Columbus's airport is pretty great as a hub and she can be anywhere in the world in about two or three days."

"I knew a woman who worked for Marriott, once," Mr. Singh said. "Anyway, we ordered the pizza before we left, it should be arriving any minute now," Mr. Singh announced. His voice was amazing. It made everyone shrink away from him a little. The sheer manliness of it would have been bullying all on its own, but it was accompanied by a tone of condescending apology, as if to say, "I'm sorry for being so much more of a man than any of you are, but that's the way it goes. I'm larger and more virile and if Darwin held any sway in human affairs your genes would be washed out of the pool, but lucky we're all more civilized than that, eh?"

"It's already here," my dad said. "Arrived a couple of minutes ago."

"I am so sorry. Please let me reimburse you," Mr. Singh pleaded, pulling his wallet from his pocket and opening it. "Ah, no cash. I'll get my checkbook from the car."

My dad waved his hands in front of himself in an oddly girlish gesture, one I'd never seen him do before. "No. It's fine. It's nice to meet you. Please come in."

Mr. Singh and my dad got the two clean plates and Gary and I used paper towels. The pizza boxes flapped open on the dining room table and Mr. Singh sat down at the head of the table.

"I'm sorry for the mess," my dad said. He gestured to the mound of books and files and loose sheets of paper nearly moldering at the other end of the table.

"No, no," Mr. Singh admonished. "It's a lovely house you have here."

"Just wish I could keep it from being consumed by papers."

"You're an academic." Mr. Singh laughed. "You don't have time for order or any of that small-minded nonsense. Too many big ideas exploding all the time, eh?" He put his fingers at his temple and made them pop away from his head.

My dad sucked his fingers clean after pulling several slices onto his plate. "Something like that," he said. "My son tells me you're a lawyer."

I snorted and Gary kicked me under the table.

Mr. Singh shot a glance at his son and then explained that he was a mechanical engineer. "I'm working at Bettle Brothers currently, helping them with their operations."

"I walk by their building every morning and have no idea what they do," Dad said.

"Well, not much goes on in that building. What the Bettle Brothers do is containers. Large plastic or cardboard drums. But here's where they are brilliant. They make nothing on site. They contract with companies and build mini-factories right next to their factories, producing what the company needs when they need it. No shipping costs, no warehousing, no extras sitting around doing nothing. It is quite brilliant. Terrifically exciting to work with such an innovative company."

Mr. Singh's Indian accent was buried underneath all the British-ness of his English. His posture was perfect and he leaned towards the person he talked to, like he was a hawk pausing before he snatched up a mouse.

"The contracting company recoups the startup cost within three years and it's all savings and convenience for them from then on to eternity."

"Sounds great," Dad said. "You've got me sold."

Mr. Singh laughed. "Maybe we will set up a fabrication plant here on your lawn. Package your ideas, your articles, your philosophies."

"Yes," Dad said, laughing as well. "I could use some philosophy boxes."

"We would need containers for the big ideas as well as the wee ones." Mr. Singh opened another beer and sipped the foam off, some of it nestling in his mustache.

"All that's left is the delivery mechanism," Dad said, opening another beer as well. He was one ahead of Mr. Singh. When he drank his posture got worse. He was always a sloucher but alcohol made his shoulders tip forward far enough so his chest was a bowl, looking like he'd just been punched in the solar plexus.

"Well, we could employ birds to deliver any thoughts you have on the environment." Mr. Singh slapped his knee at his own joke.

"And moles," Gary said. "Y'know, for his deep ideas."

Everyone laughed at this. The table was suddenly tense with everyone trying to think up another method, another joke. Angels for his eschatological thoughts? "Do Not Open: Alive/Dead Cat Inside" stickers for his Schrodinger's boxes? Leather strops for his line of Occam's razors? Special felt-bottom shoes for his mirror stages? Return to Sender stamps for the Socratic method? My mind wheeled with jokes, but I didn't say any of them. Mr. Singh was still laughing, even after everyone else had stopped. It was like he was having a fit.

Gary put his hand on his Mr. Singh's shoulder. "Dad? You okay?"

Little tears squirted out of the corners of his eyes. "It's so funny. I am sorry. It's just that the joke here is that you really produce absolutely nothing. Wait. Wait." Mr. Singh gulped at his beer. "We could use balloons for all the hot air you spew out."

"Hey," my dad said. "Hey."

"You have this beautiful house and you make nothing, you create nothing, you don't even have your own ideas." Mr. Singh was laughing so hard he was having a hard time breathing. "You make a living off of the ideas of others."

"I'm sorry," Gary said. "He shouldn't drink. He's got no tolerance for it."

"Oh, be quiet," Mr. Singh said. "We're all having fun here. I'm merely pointing out, for the record, that our host, our dear, dear host, is useless. His wife is the breadwinner and he's the nanny taking care of that one, the Yo-Yo Fag, is it? The troublemaker." He jabbed a finger in my direction. "His philosophy? It's like a little hobby for him."

My father's face was ashen. His lips quivered, there were too many things he wanted to say—there was a logjam at his mouth. His life's work had been sucker punched.

"I think it's time you left," I said.

"C'mon. I'm the soberest one here," Mr. Singh said, after regaining a modicum of composure. He stood up. Gary did as well and shadowed his old man. "You can take a joke. He can take a joke." He patted my dad on his head. "It's all in fun. Just taking the piss out of your old man."

"Please leave," I said.

Gary grabbed his dad's hand and led him around the table. Mr. Singh shook him off. There was a family picture on the north wall. Mom, Dad, and me. Sears studio. Fake library screen behind us. Mr. Singh gazed at it for a minute. He reached out to touch the picture but his hand just hovered there, finger nearly grazing my mom's face. He shook his head.

"C'mon, Gurbaksh," he yelled. He got to the door of the dining room. "I'm sorry if you thought I was being rude. Sorry if you took offense. I was just playing, eh?" He then performed an elaborate curtsy, picking up his shirt's tails like they were his skirt. No one laughed. "In Budweiser Veritas," he muttered, then giggled. He walked outside, leaving the door wide open.

"I'm really sorry about this. He had a couple of beers before we left. He was nervous about meeting you and your dad," Gary said to me. There was humiliation on his face, but there was also fatigue. This wasn't the first time his dad had done this. "I'm sorry, Dr. Nadler. My dad's kind of a jackass."

My dad sat there silent. His mouth still doing that quivering logjam thing.

"I'll see you on Monday," Gary said. He hugged me then followed his dad, closing the door gently behind him.

I cleaned up the pizza boxes. Put the remaining slices into ziplocks and into the fridge. I crushed the beer cans. Washed the glasses. Stuffed the two-liters into the garbage. At some point my father disappeared into his office. I didn't see him the rest of the night.

I went outside and watched the stars for a while. My heart was racing. I know I should've been worried about my dad but another thing had occurred to me: I hadn't been hugged by someone my own age since kindergarten.

I actually had a friend.

CHAPTER 14

THE WEEKEND DRIBBLED out of my fingers and suddenly I was waiting for the bus again. People called me "Yo-Yo Fag" as they got on the bus, but it seemed like there was a little bit of deference in their voices.

At school, on the shiny spot on my locker where I'd cleaned the drawing off, was this:

Faggot!!!

By this time, I was on a first-name basis with the janitor. His name for real was Tiny. It had probably started out as a nickname that he'd accepted with hope that acceptance would lessen its sting. It was written on his sewn-on badge in cursive. He had a set of keys to a door that led downstairs, into which he'd go and come back with the steel bucket, gloves, steel wool, and spray cleaner.

"Don't let that splash back into your eyes," he said, poking at the bottle. He could've been anywhere from forty-five to seventy. He was under five feet but seemed like he had extra skin, and only lacked the willpower to grow into it. He looked like Jimmy Durante—sad, beat up, worn down, giant nose, in the bottle. He shuffled when he walked, which led one to notice how his jumpsuit pants were cuffed several times over to accommodate his stature. He stuttered when he talked. He stuttered and he shuffled and he worked at a high school. The poor son of a bitch.

I wanted to get away from him as soon as possible.

My wrist hurt from scrubbing my locker. The central patch of it shone brighter than ever. Probably even more than when it was first installed. I think I'd gotten down to the unfinished steel of it.

There were rumors that the room down the stairs where Tiny got his cleaning products from led to a network of tunnels built during the Underground Railroad days. People at my school believed that the Underground Railroad was literally beneath the earth, which might be the grandest act of imagination they ever committed. The tunnel myth persisted maybe because Tiny kind of looked like a mole person, someone always blinking in the bright lights of the aboveground world. And maybe when people see a shuffler, a stumbler, a guy with a big nose pushing a broom and cleaning up teenagers' puke, the natural reaction I think is to imagine via the negative capability what realm he rules in his off time. Off the clock, down the stairs, out of his jumpsuit, was Tiny, lord of the mole people, ruler of all that happens underneath Rutherford, Ohio?

Or maybe he had a pretty good marriage that ended too quickly.

I knocked on his door to return the cleaning products. He was sitting on a bucket, smoking a cigarette, underlining stuff in a *Reader's Digest*. He nodded at the bare space near his feet.

CHAPTER 15

OHIO HISTORY WAS A MANDATORY CLASS for all freshmen. It was pretty much all about the locks on the Erie Canal, the Pro Football Hall of Fame, Branch Rickey, and Rutherford B. Hayes. It was unlikely that even in February we'd talk about Paul Dunbar. It'd be a special kind of pleasure to watch Mr. Tyler, the Junior High School Wrestling and Assistant Football Coach, read and parse out "We Wear the Mask."

He had wavy black hair and giant glasses, which made his brown eyes look cowish. His skin was the color of whatever comes out of zits when you squeeze them. He wore white polo shirts tucked into slacks of the three male colors: dark blue, gray, and black. Mr. Tyler liked to lean back in his chair with his hands behind his head and talk about his truck, all the modifications he'd done to it. We were supposed to memorize all of the eighty-eight counties in Ohio by the end of the term. He had used the same test for twelve years. He still had the paddle he made for the now-illegal spankings. It sat on the chalkboard. Six inches wide with a series of holes drilled in it to make it whistle through the air when he spanked someone who'd broken one of his rules. The real insult was the handle wrapped in the cushion tape used on tennis rackets; beating you wouldn't hurt his hands.

He told us at the beginning of the quarter to feel free to call him "Coach." No one took him up on it. In a small town, in a small district, you know so much about a teacher before you ever have him. Mr. Tyler was a lifelong bachelor. Thirty-five or -six, he'd talk about his dating life in class. He had a famous story about a time when a woman he was dating for a long time, three months or so—divorced woman, three kids—asked him if he had ever smoked "Mary Jane," and then he'd tell us that that was slang for marijuana. They were at dinner and he walked out on her without saying a word. He left her at the restaurant to get her own ride home, to pay the bill. He told this story to his classes. He wanted us to know how righteous he was. How anti-drug he was. He bragged about how the woman kept calling and how he had to call the phone company to block her number. He also let his classes know in a whisper that there might have been an anonymous phone call or two to the police as well as to Child Protective Services, tipping them off to a drug user in their area.

It was the only class that Gary and I had together. Word was Mr. Tyler had led the opposition to the corporal punishment ban and gave some impassioned speeches to the school board. He told them that they were cutting off a teacher's arm and replacing it with a pile of detention slips. This was the guy who didn't talk about Cincinnati's role in the Underground Railroad, didn't talk about Dayton's crazy position as the Paris of Ohio, and brushed over the fact that Marietta was the first capital of Ohio. Nothing mattered other than memorizing the counties and writing a three-page essay on the importance of the Erie Canal.

That day we were coloring the different counties different colors. We each had a partial set of colored pencils and there was constantly a line at the pencil sharpener because the things broke so easily. I was coloring mine according to the metaphysical exports each county produces. Ottawa County I shaded brown and then erased it and colored it white to represent its existential irony as a place named after the people whose land was stolen, same with Erie, Miami, and Delaware counties. Lucas County, home of Toledo, was the color of an abscess. And Cuyahoga County, home of Cleveland, was green—(poor Cleveland doesn't know if it wants to secede from Ohio or if Ohio wants to secede from it). Akron was rust, the color of the belt that's strangling it. For Dayton I tried to find a color in all of the crappy ancient cast-off colors that represented how Dayton is the prettiest girl at a pretty hideous ball—poor Dayton, which has produced more culture than the rest of the state combined but everyone thinks is just race riots and tires. Gallia County, poor Gallia county, whose name means "France" in Latin, was colored burnt umber since that color sounds classy. Ashtabula, I put four red dots to represent the dead at Kent State. I left Rutherford blank.

At the end of class, Mr. Tyler asked everyone to come up and show off their maps. The little redheaded girl from the bus was first; I didn't even know she was in our class. She had brought her own colored pencils and her map was crisply colored, the counties clearly defined.

"That's what I'm talking about," Mr. Meyers crowed and thumb-tacked her map to the bulletin board. The redheaded girl squirmed under the attention. Mr. Meyers jerked a thumb at her map and said, "This is what it means to take pride in your work. Good job." And here Mr. Tyler pulled himself away to read his gradebook to get her name. "Miss, uh, Jarvis, this is great work. Attention to detail. That's what gets you ahead in life." He didn't mention of course that she had used her own materials rather than the stubby broken pencils he'd provided.

According to the eighteen-inch wall clock's jerky second arm, class was at the very cusp of ending. Students started to stuff things in backpacks. The class rustled with anticipation.

"Stop," Mr. Tyler slapped his hand on the blackboard. "I dismiss you. Not the bell. This is my class, my rules. I want all you losers to know what it takes to succeed in life. Miss Jarvis here has . . ."

The bell rang and in the middle of him praising her, she vanished. She had fled. She was a ninja. It was astonishing. How had she done it? The door had been closed, for Christ's sake.

Mr. Tyler hadn't seen her leave either and now his mouth hung agape. "Dismissed," he muttered.

CHAPTER 16

IN ENGLISH CLASS, the mousy Mr. Morris handed out paperback copies of *The Great Gatsby* and announced that we'd be spending the next six weeks reading it. It was a tiny book, something an illiterate person could finish in a long weekend and we'd be spending a month and a half on. He passed out shopping bags next. The rest of the period was to be spent making a cover for the book. He had three scissors for the entire class and two boxes of crayons borrowed from the art class. Most teachers had us cover our books as a homework assignment so this said something about the state of affairs in Mr. Morris's lesson plans. This was the laziest busywork.

Mr. Morris had been sick recently, coughing and such, so maybe that's why he was phoning it in.

After hearing everyone effuse about *Gatsby* as *the* American novel, I'd read it in sixth grade. As a love story, it was lacking. Unless it was people in love with themselves. Daisy was in love not with Gatsby but with the way Gatsby saw her. And Gatsby was in love with being worthy of Daisy. No one was in love with Tom. Even Myrtle wasn't in love with Tom but with the opportunity she saw in him. She could escape her crappy marriage and the valley of ashes she found herself wallowing in. And Tom liked Myrtle because of how she looked at him and because she was disposable. The only real love story was Jordan Baker and Nick Carraway and Nick doesn't even realize that she's in love with him. Everyone is so oblivious. It's just hard to buy that adults are that unaware.

Normally I'd love a book that cynical. But I'm not sure it's meant to be that cynical. It's written in such pretty prose and that prettiness doesn't seem to carry its negativity. Like a pair of brass knuckles in wet paper towels. Also it might be full of the absolute shittiest "symbols" in all of high school English classes. The green light Gatsby is always staring at, Dr. T. J. Eckleburg's billboard, the clock Gatsby almost knocks over in Nick's little house when he sees Daisy again (objective correlative much?). Like *The Scarlet Letter*, it might be the Great American Novel because it's easy to teach.

The best thing about Gatsby is the cover. The weirdo face hanging above the streaks of nighttime traffic. If we're going to have to write a book report on this thing, which, if we're going to spend six weeks on it, is a guarantee, I want to write about the cover. It's haunting. But that's what we were tasked with covering up in our first lesson.

"Barry, you're daydreaming again," Mr. Morris called from his desk. He was picking at these purple dots on his scalp, old man zits or something. "Please catch up with the rest of the class. C'mon, cover your book."

I finished covering it in five minutes. I spent the rest of the class making a detailed crayon drawing of Myrtle Wilson getting hit by Gatsby's car, a drawing which would almost guarantee another trip to the guidance counselor.

Fuck English class.

CHAPTER 17

BEING POPULAR was not what I expected.

But I wasn't popular. I was infamous. There's a pretty big difference there. Like Greg Prince was already popular before he and his girlfriend stole his parents' car and drove to North Carolina to follow the Grateful Dead. Then he became infamous, which made him more popular. He already had a base of popularity on which to build off of. People were invested in the Greg Prince narrative and so when this extreme thing happened people loved him more. He was exciting. Unpredictable. And that unpredictability was added to his already long list of popular traits. It was like putting a hot pepper into chocolate. A new twist on something already beloved.

I was a hot pepper. Just a hot pepper. If anything I was a hot pepper put into oatmeal.

Gary was popular now. In part because he was infamous-adjacent. He had that particular talent of being socially alchemical. He could turn the shit I had done in Mrs. Gildea's office into gold. He could tell the story of that day in her office, of me breaking her pictures, of me screaming at her, of me being suspended, better than I could. People liked him for that story; people were wary of me for that same thing.

It was weird to me that Gary was so popular so quickly, given how racist and shitty Rutherford generally was. I asked him about it.

"I don't know what to tell you. There must be a reason the English used us as policemen in India, Hong Kong, and Shanghai, but I don't know it. Maybe we're seen as self-contained and honorable in our otherness," Gary said. "Also I'm deathly charming, man."

I was now popular-adjacent. And that was its own thing. I had someone to sit with at lunch and that someone could sit at nearly any table he wanted. Upperclassmen, underclassmen, wrestlers, the Dungeons & Dragons/Comic Book dudes, cheerleaders, the dudes playing their millionth hand of euchre—it was all a buffet for Gary. And I got to sit with him. I got to sit next to Cheri Dantz, she of the cheerleading team and gymnastics team, a homecoming court staple, poofed hair and shoulder pads. I'd jerked off to her in her yearbook picture for close to three years now. That Cheri Dantz. I got to sit next to her. I got to watch her eat an apple.

I was quiet. I was a creep. But now that's what people expected of me, what they wanted from me. And it's not like I needed to talk anyway. Gary was always in motion, always performing, always entertaining. He stood out, brown-skinned with his headwrap and topknot—a version of the Sikh turban called a "patka"—but he stood out mostly for how he blended in. He was fluent in *clique*, if that's possible. His brownness and his turban gave him a pass; it seemed that everyone embraced him because he wasn't a threat. Not one of the black guys, with their loud music no one understood and everyone was afraid of. Not one of the Future Farmer white guys, with their weary "I helped a horse give birth before I came to school" look. Not one of the D&D guys with their black shirts and obscure references. Not one of the pretty girls who always seemed so nervous, as if they were playing high-risk poker, wary that someone had seen their hand.

Gary was his own clique. And I was Gary's best friend.

Everyone loved Gary Singh.

CHAPTER 18

IT WAS AT SOME PARTY. Not that first party at Meggie Morrison's house or the one at Tiffany Ichida's house either. Maybe it was at Kyle Louden's house. I was losing track already. The parties were mostly all the same to me. I sat in a corner quietly. If there was a TV, I turned it on. We didn't have one so it was always a weird experience watching TV, a strange window into all of these worlds I didn't know existed: *Facts of Life, Gimme a Break!, Down to Earth, Mama's Family, Hee-Haw, Soul Train, Star Search*—it was a parallel culture running right alongside mine, like an underground river, that I could dangle my toes in until the party got busted.

Parties always got busted.

What teenager actually thinks they can have forty friends over, drinking alcohol in the front yard, blasting Michael Jackson from the house speakers turned towards the backyard, yelling at one another as they peeled out in their parent's cars, and not get caught? The world is a system of people watching each other and ratting each other out. So either the neighbors would call, or someone who didn't get invited would call, or the person having the party would call because they suddenly realized what a terrible idea this was in the first place.

Sometimes it took a couple hours before things got out of hand. I'd find the den or the rumpus room or the game room or the living room or the finished basement and watch TV until then. Gary would be upstairs. He didn't drink but he always kept a cup in his hand so people thought he was drinking. He said it was a lot more fun watching people be fools than being a fool yourself. What pleasure a person could get from other people's bad decisions I didn't know. But I also didn't ask. I didn't know what pleasure people got out of most of the things they did: sports, popular music, McDonald's. It all was the same dull paste to me.

So I don't remember which party, but I do remember that I was watching an *A-Team* rerun when a girl slumped onto the couch next to me.

"Anything good on?" she asked.

"This," I said, pointing at the screen. B. A. Baracus was being tranquilized by his boss because he was afraid of flying. The fact that a black man was being drugged in order to be put into transit so that he could do a job some other place clearly had echoes of the slave trade. "Black man, use your incomprehensible body to do something for us!" All shows had the same kind of message. Even if there wasn't a black person on-screen, there was always a fairly clear "us." The "us" that clearly needed cheaper Mop & Glo, newer cars with Corinthian leather, Cola taste tests, space-age technology, and elaborate euphemisms for any fluid coming out of a woman. Hegel says an Englishman can take what you call pleasure and convince you that it's not pleasure at all, but a new pleasure is just around the corner with these new products. The world will promise you things for senses you don't have. TV might as well promise you X-ray vision, the ability to taste radio waves, or a paste that would create new erogenous zones on your calloused flesh. It was all the same shit destined for the landfill. I was smart enough not to say any of this to the girl. "It's okay," I said.

"I'm Ottilie."

"Barry." I didn't turn to look at her. If she was beautiful, I'd become stupid. If she was ugly, I'd put up defenses. It was better not knowing what she looked like in order to have a real conversation. Better to just catch her in my periphery. She had a name, a hell of a name. And there wasn't a pseudonym, an exonym. She just had a weird name.

"Why are you watching TV instead of being part of the group?"

"I don't know," I said, but I said it as one word: idunno, more of an exhalation than words, like a word loaf being excreted from my mouth.

"I don't know anyone here," she said. "I mean, I came with some people and they know people, the people who are throwing the party, I guess, but I don't know anyone but the people I came with so they're all off talking to people they know and here I am talking to you."

"Sorry," I said.

There was a gunfight on the screen, the tips of the Uzis writing exploding cursive in the air.

"What's your favorite white cheese?" Ottilie asked.

"What?"

"I am making an effort. It's called small talk, I'm trying to get better at it, but I need someone to practice making it with," she said and then laughed. "Making the small talk with I mean. Not 'making it with' like a baby, a cake, or sex or anything."

"Cheddar," I said.

"Hah!" she shouted. "But incorrect. Cheddar is orange."

"There are white cheddars," I said.

"I do not believe you. I have never seen a white cheddar." She clapped her hands. "See, we're making small talk. I like feta. I'd eat it all day if I wouldn't get like huge or anything."

"What's wrong with huge?"

"Says the guy who believes in white cheddar."

"There are white cheddars."

"Do you believe in sasquatch too? Yetis? Fairies? Orcs?"

"You read Tolkien?" I asked, still not looking at her. Now I was in too deep to suddenly look over at her. When I looked at her whatever my eyes said would be everything. If I found her attractive she'd know it; if I thought she was ugly she'd know it. I should've looked at her when she first sat down.

"Just *The Hobbit*. I can't get through the first book in *The Lord of the Rings*."

"Where'd you stop?"

"They were at Tom Bombadil's house."

"It gets better."

"That's what people say. That's what people always say. But he's like this gross big fat hippie version of Falstaff and it just feels dumb and small and I can't trust a writer who spends so much time on a bad imitation." Ottilie shifted her position on the couch. I could feel her weight on the couch. "See, we're doing it. We're talking. My uncle was right."

"Your uncle?"

"My uncle, well he's not really my uncle, he's my dad's best friend. Do adults have best friends? Do we ever age out of ranking our relationships? Anyway, Uncle Scott says that you can start up a conversation with anyone by asking about their favorite white cheese. It's because everyone has an opinion. Everyone has a favorite white cheese and the question is benign because no one could ever think someone had an ulterior motive with a cheese question. Uncle Scott says it disarms people, wiggles past their defenses, and you end up in a conversation as a result."

"Nice," I said. "Except for vegans."

Ottilie laughed. "No one wants to talk to a vegan."

I laughed and looked at her. It was involuntary. I turn my head sometimes when I laugh. The thing my brain wouldn't let me do, my body did. She had a purple long-sleeve t-shirt knotted on the side so you could see a little bit of her belly. It said Duran Duran on it. She had brown curly hair piled on her head by some architectural principle I couldn't fathom. She had brown eyes and acne and her laugh sounded like a screech owl going in for the kill. I didn't know if she was attractive but I didn't want her to leave.

"Baruch," I said.

"What's that?"

"My name." A moment of silence fell between us. "I'm named after Baruch Spinoza the philosopher."

"I'm named after Ottilie Assing, the suffragist who had an affair with Frederick Douglass."

"That's pretty good," I said.

"I don't know. When she found out that Douglass married his secretary she committed suicide."

"I've never been able to read anything by Spinoza. I keep trying because it's my name and everything but I can't make sense of it at all."

"I think my mom named me this because she's a white lady who married a black man."

"So she named you after herself in a way?"

"Yes. Not literally but in spirit."

"Damn," I said. "That's heavy. You win at the weird-name game."

"I would've won anyway," she said, taking me in in a quick glance away from the TV. "You hide your weird name."

"I guess I do. It is a little much though for small-town Ohio."

She stood up and stretched her arms behind her back. "One of my goals in life is to be too much for small-town Ohio."

CHAPTER 19

PARTIES. LIKE I SAID, a terrible idea. Teenagers, alcohol, your parents' stuff. What the heck could go right?

But you could also meet Ottilie, who went to Olentangy, which was the kind of school parents' moved near for their kids' education. Not private, just self-selecting. She gave me her number.

And then the party was busted. I knew that because kids started running through the house screaming, "We're busted. We're busted."

I snuck out using the sliding patio door and I hopped over the balcony railing and took off through the woods in the back of the house. I ran and ran. At some point I was well clear of the cops but I kept running. It was its own pleasure. The air was cold and it rushed into my lungs and made my skin feel like it was radiating energy. I was sweating and cold at the same time and I kept running. The sodium lights of the mini-malls and the grocery stores and the gas stations and the hospital all caught my profile and cast my shadow to stretch out into the night. It was sort of like my panic moments. I couldn't stop, my chest was pounding, my thoughts were racing, but it felt good. It felt great. My windbreaker ballooned out behind me with the cold wind blowing through town. At the end of downtown, I executed a left turn, punctuated with a soldier's pivot. Hard 90 degrees. My arms pumping. My legs weightless. My lungs lovely. Was I a brilliant runner? How fast was I going? Did I have this ability my whole life and not know it? I ran all the way home without stopping. All those years of skipping Kill Ball to run laps on the creaky catwalk around the gym suddenly felt like genius preparation for this night. This cold night in late September—the leaves rustling and crunching in the yards I cut through on my way home, the smell of burnt leaves in the air, the smell of wet leaves decomposing coming from the ground. I was giddy. The nerves, the tension, the spine-snapping energy I sat on all day every day put to use pushing my legs, levering my arms, moving me through the central Ohio agrarian darkness of the harvest. This was Peter Parker when he was bit by the radioactive spider. Scott Summers waking up in the orphanage and his optic beams blowing the roof off of the thing. Hank McCoy executing the triple flip to avoid being hit by a car. Hal Jordan realizing what the alien's green ring could really do. John Glenn on his first orbit around the moon. I had power I didn't know I had. It wasn't just meeting a girl. Not just having a real conversation with a girl and having a friend. It was something else.

I got home and panted and drank two glasses of water in a second, keeping my hand on the tap while I drank the first one down.

"You're home?" my dad asked.

I nodded, continuing to pant. I wiped my mouth with my sleeve and filled my glass again. "I ran the whole way, Dad. It was like five miles. Maybe tomorrow we can go out in the car and track it with the odometer." I wanted to tell my dad how fast I was, how my legs were miracles grafted onto me, ask him if he knew any coaches at the college who might be interested in me.

"You were at the Singh's. It's not five miles to the Singh's." My dad peeled his glasses off, his voice deepened into the punishment octaves. "And where's your bike?"

"I left it at the Singh's." Why was my dad giving a shit about these specifics? I had developed a new power. We should be celebrating.

"Where have you been?"

"There was a party. But Dad, I think I'm a really good runner."

The phone rang. My dad walked to get it off the wall. He stumbled a little and I noticed he had been carrying a glass of scotch with him. It wasn't a short glass either, but one of the water glasses.

"Yeah," he said into the receiver. "He's here, Gary." Dad squared his eyes at me and made sure I was watching him talk. "No, you can't speak with him. Because he's grounded." Dad took a swig of his scotch, the ice cubes somersaulting on the way back down. "No, I don't. Your dad was here earlier, but I don't know where he went. I can't keep track of my own son. I can't keep track of anyone."

Pause. Swig.

"I'm not going to tell your dad. Unless he asks. I keep secrets but I won't lie. Not for you anyway."

Pause. Swig. The glass was empty! Dad held it up to the light like something suspicious had happened. He squinted at it. *Where had all that scotch gone?* he seemed to be asking himself.

"Whatever. You still can't talk to him. Wait for school, Gary. Bye-bye."

Dad missed the cradle hanging the phone up. It was wall-mounted and had a smooth dolphin curve. Dad hung it up upside down and laughed like he'd done something no one had thought of before. He turned to me, shook his empty glass by his ear, and said, "I am celebrating."

"Mr. Singh was here?"

Dad walked to the fridge and opened the cabinet above it. He pulled out the handle of Cutty Sark and filled his glass. "What are you celebrating, Dad?" he said in a falsetto. He opened the fridge and twisted ice cubes free from the plastic tray.

"Mr. Singh was a total dick to you. Now you're buddies?"

"Well, son. Since you asked. I am celebrating many things. Three things, really. Number one is that I got a job."

"The college hired you? Full time?"

My dad shook his head. "Get a glass for yourself."

"I'm fine."

"Get a glass and have a drink with me. You can't go off to secret parties and then come home and refuse to drink with your dad."

He burped. He was cartoonishly drunk. Like Andy Capp–drunk. I expected him to start saying "hic, hic, hic" anytime now. I got a glass. A short one. He slopped it half full.

"Want ice? You're not supposed to drink scotch with ice. It makes the taste buds contract." He tapped his head three times. "I've got a PhD; I know things." He capped the bottle and tossed two ice cubes in my glass. "But when you're drinking shitty scotch it doesn't matter." Dad and I clinked glasses. He stared me in the eyes. His eyes were glacier blue. They were haunting, just enough pigment in them to make them a color. They seemed even paler tonight, like something inside him was calving. He took a large gulp from his glass. I took a swallow and immediately regretted it.

Dad patted me on my back as I coughed and spat into the sink. "It's a burn, right? That burn is life. Alcohol, it's poison. Your body is smart to reject poison." He took another gulp from his glass. "It gets easier though once you get a taste for it." He walked into the living room. I followed. I brought my glass of scotch with me. In our living room there was a couch and a recliner. Dad collapsed on the couch.

"Doc," he said. "I have to tell you about my dreams." He laughed at his own joke. He looked up at me.

"Dad, you got hired by the college?"

"Doc, these dreams—they've been torturing me for a long time, y'know." Dad had adopted a hick accent that gleamed with sincerity. When I didn't laugh, Dad grimaced. I was letting him down by not finding him hilarious. He sighed. "No, boy. I did not get hired by the college. I am pursuing a new career."

"But your book?"

"Why write about something nobody cares about so no one can buy it? Everyone else in the world, it's like making money is this talent, this ability that I never learned. There's so much money, I want some of it."

"We're fine. Mom's salary, I thought . . ." Dad gave me a look that stopped that sentence.

"I'm starting at Bettle Brothers on Monday," he said.

"But your classes."

"Fuck 'em," he said and laughed. "Fuck 'em. Like they give a damn about me."

"You're going to quit midterm? Won't that like blacklist you or something?"

The fan spun at full speed above us. I noticed it was freezing in the room. Dad had opened all of the windows. The sweat from my run was sending a chill I felt in my spine all the way down to my butt. How had I not noticed it was freezing? I took a sip of my scotch. It was awful but it did make me feel warmer.

"So the first thing we're celebrating is my new job." Dad hoisted his glass in the air, clinking glasses with the wall art. "The second thing we're celebrating is your dad giving up." He turned to me. "People will tell you, Barry, that you should pursue your passion, that you should do what you love, that it'll be hard but if you commit yourself, really commit yourself to what you love, then the world will open up, blossom for you." Dad drank. Dad coughed. Dad winced. "It's bullshit. Today we're celebrating the death of the dream, the death of your dad's delusions. Those people who tell you about following your dream are always sitting on a pile of money. I want my pile of money." Dad laughed and drank again. He coughed again. A minute went by and he was snoring.

Consider the drunk father, passed out on the couch, his legs akimbo, his arms—one on his crotch, his hand intermittently scratching his balls, as if the hand worked independently of the rest of the father system, a little butler who tidied up while the master was asleep, scratching the balls like whisking ashes into a dustpan, the other arm off the couch, trailing in the nap of the shag carpet, like a fisherman letting his fingers dangle in the lake as the boat steered itself, as the line's bobbin bobbed in the water, waiting and wanting/not wanting a fish to take the bait. His stomach was showing. He'd gained more weight than I had thought. His big mottled hairy belly was a new tenant with its own demands. Our house had recently never lacked for ice cream or cheese.

What's your favorite white cheese? Maybe she was attractive. Maybe when you can't stop thinking about someone that's when they're attractive. Maybe it wasn't about attractiveness at all. Maybe it was just about who you couldn't stop thinking about.

I met a girl. I ran what had to be five miles. And I came home to my dad drunk enough that he passed out while telling me he'd quit being a professor. I didn't think it was legal to quit in the middle of a semester. I grabbed my two glasses and my dad's glass. I ditched the scotch glasses in the sink and refilled my water glass. My legs were still a little trembly from the run.

The kitchen smelled like scotch and farts. It was a celebration! I almost cleaned up because I knew Dad would feel awful in the morning but then I decided against it for that same reason. He'd feel so bad, it'd probably be good for him to have some chores to do. He'd made himself some microwave grilled cheeses and the residue inside the open microwave was a charry bubbly slag of burnt bagged shredded cheese. I picked at it and it came off in a single greasy shingle. I put the cheese on top of his scotch glass in the sink. It was a celebration!

Dad had quit his job. Dad had gotten a new one at the place Mr. Singh worked. But he said there were three things he was celebrating. Had he told me what the third one was and I missed it? I grabbed the bread and bagged cheese and made to put them away when I noticed the index card taped to the fridge.

Delta 431: 8:35 pm was written in sharpie. With three exclamation points after it.

I knew the third thing now.

Mom was coming home.

CHAPTER 20

MOM GOT OUT OF COLLEGE and worked for IBM. She was a sales something or other. Mostly what she told about those days was getting to travel and having to wear white gloves all the time. She grew up in Wisconsin, the second daughter of a truck farmer who had a son and a daughter after her. I never met the man but there were enough equivocations and euphemisms to describe him ("He was a good man, tough but good"; "Alcohol certainly didn't enhance his parenting"; "He came from the old school of raising kids"; "He believed in discipline"; "Very Old Testament") that it was perfectly clear he'd beaten the kids growing up. Mom was close to her mom. When Mom was in college, she found out her mom died and my mom went in to take a math test. She can do that. Compartmentalize, I mean. Her insides can be at high tide but she always has a placid look. The joke we make is that she's half Norwegian and half Vulcan.

She met Dad in Cleveland. He was finishing his PhD on a student deferment. It was at a bar. He invited her to a party at his apartment the next week. My mom agreed. And she brought a date to that party. My dad figured either she was clueless or she was cruel and drank himself sad that night.

He called her the next morning and told her he really liked her and it was rude to bring that guy and he was sorry that he was making such a big deal of it. This is important. My dad called to harangue her and ended up apologizing—this is my dad. I've never been grounded without him lifting it a day later. He's a sucker, a mark, a sap. But maybe that's what she liked about him. They had lunch. They got married. And here's my equivocation: they came from a different time, so even though Mom kept her maiden name, she quit IBM to follow Dad's academic career. Dad taught in Omaha, then in Bismarck, Flagstaff, Denton, then in Wheeling, then he got the position here. He was feted when he first arrived. Gave a public reading; a faculty cocktail party in his honor; designed his own upperclassman classes; was given course relief so he could write his book on translating Hegel; health insurance; 401k; dinner at the president's house every semester; a profile in the local paper and an interview with the Columbus Dispatch. The appointment was for three years and was meant to give junior faculty a place to launch their careers. But after that third year, my dad stayed. You know how you can dress up as Batman on Halloween and everyone plays along but if you are still wearing the costume November 1, you're a lunatic? Dad had been dressing up as professor for fourteen years.

I was born in Wheeling, so his course relief was spent running after me, not publishing, writing, or looking for another job. He was politely demoted to visiting professor and then to adjunct faculty. They took his office from him, they gave the classes he designed to senior faculty, and only gave him Intro classes. Another young professor came in for the three-year appointment—that guy they hired after two years. That guy frequently asked my dad for advice in the beginning and now condescended to him: "Tough job market out there. We didn't become philosophers to get rich." Ha ha ha ha.

Dickhead.

But Dad kept having him over for drinks every couple of weeks. He was probably the closest thing Dad had to a friend.

Once I got into school, Mom got bored. She took classes at OSU. She got her MBA. She got a degree in Hotel Restaurant Management.

She got hired by Marriott. Now her normal business trip takes her out of the house for three weeks at a time. This time she's been gone for seven.

We waited at her gate. Dad brought flowers; I talked him out of a box of candy. Dad was more nervous than I'd seen him in a while. And it was in his pacing, his bumming of a cigarette off of a stranger, his botched attempts at lighting up, that I realized he didn't talk to Mom before quitting the college.

The ride home was going to suck.

Mom came out of the gangway with her sleep mask around her neck and three bags clustered around her. She had a purple blouse on and a black pleated skirt. She always dressed up for flights, even overnight ones. "You never know when they're going to bump you to first class," was one of her adages. Her hair was a mess but she had freshly applied makeup and she stank of mouthwash. Dad messed up their hug by trying to hug her first when Mom went for the flowers. It looked like she was disarming an attacker. They laughed. Mom snatched the flowers from him and hugged him. And then she hugged me. The spectacular ergonomics of a mom's hug. I suddenly wanted to tell her about Ottilie and my special running power and my new friend Gary and drinking scotch with Dad and being infamous but not popular and how there was a difference between the two. My throat got that tight feeling and my thoughts were going like a broken carousel, spinning and spinning—the brake snapped, the gears loosening, all of it fit to fly away.

The way she smelled made me want to tell her everything. The mouthwash, old perfume, slept-in-clothes smell. This was Mom smell.

And every time I smelled it I was reminded that I was an unrepentant pansy-assed mama's boy. I loved her like a lemming loves another lemming's rear end. Maybe it was her hair, chestnut brown to her shoulders in something called a demi-wave, or the fact that she liked to eat popcorn while she did the crossword or because she had never once tried to explain Kierkegaard to me. I grabbed two of her carry-ons and started to hustle ahead of them. She never checked luggage. She hated airports that much. She would rather wear the same thing over and over than stay the twenty extra minutes waiting for the baggage to be unloaded. They were walking slowly, so I hustled back, making a joke of running circles around them. Let's get to the car, let's get on the highway, let's get home. I wanted to wake up and have Mom smell in the house.

"You're smoking now," she said to dad.

Dad looked at the cigarette in his hand like a pickpocket had placed it there. He tossed it on the airport floor and stepped on it. "I quit teaching," he said.

He couldn't have waited for the car? He could have told her when we were driving home and then we'd still be in motion. Instead, he did it like he was swimming in a cold pond. Jumped right in. Maybe he figured hitting mom with it when she was jet-lagged would be strategic. She stopped walking and dropped my dad's hand. Everyone was in movement around us. People hoisting children. Skycaps pushing wheelchairs. Business people checking their watches. College kids carrying guitars. Even the shoe-polishing guy was in motion, his brush going whisk whisk whisk whisk.

"Are you out of your mind?" she asked. When someone says that line, you expect them—no, you *want* them—to scream it. My mom said it like Clint Eastwood. Quiet and steely.

"They were never going to hire me on full time. There was no market incentive for them to do it. Why pay me more when I was clearly willing to work for nothing? I'm done with the dream. I'm awake now and I'm going to do real work and make real money and I'll provide enough so you don't have to be gone all of the time and we can be a family."

"We are a family," my mom said. Her coldness was freaking me out. It was freaking Dad out. He started talking faster and faster.

"I've already got a new job. I didn't quit the old one before getting another one. I'm not stupid. I just had had enough of being funded by my wife, by my silly dream, my unprofitable profession, making you work and travel so much. I miss you. Barry misses you. I thought this could get you off the road as much."

"You want me to quit my job?" If she were a porcupine, her quills would be jammed so far into Dad that every major organ would be pierced. "You decided to quit your job, burning who knows how many bridges in the process, and you also decided that I would quit mine too? Were you going to talk to me about this? Maybe ask how I felt about this?"

I dropped the bags by the wall and sat next to them. People swerved around them. Happy people. Busy people. Soldiers in uniform holding hands with pregnant women.

My dad continued to talk faster and faster, he was sweeping against the wind but he couldn't stop himself. "I was tired of everyone sacrificing for me. For this stupid dream I had of being a professor, of teaching these theories about life to Econ majors who want nothing more than for me to tell them how any of this is going to profit them. They want education to be a tool and I can't do that. I'm bad at that. I teach useless things and for a long time I took pride in it, felt like I was doing soul work, forging young characters, making the world a better place one reading of *The Republic* at a time. But I can't do it anymore. It's a different world. No one wants to be smart. Everyone wants to be rich. They're sending a schoolteacher into space, but you know who's going to be next. The wealthy. They will own and experience everything. I can't fight that anymore. I'm not going to put my family in jeopardy and send my wife away for months at a time so I can just play out this dumb dream I had of being important, of being a wise man, of chasing out the knowledge hidden in plain sight, teaching others to do it."

A man driving a golf cart was yelling, "Coming through. Coming through. Move to the side. Coming through." Dad grabbed Mom by her shoulders and pulled her out of the way.

"It wasn't just your dream," she said.

She didn't say another word until we got home. She was putting back together a grenade that had gone off inside of her. Collecting the shrapnel, withdrawing it from where it had lodged.

After I'd run upstairs to floss and brush and change into my pj's, she came into my bedroom. "You should've told me about this, Baruch," she said.

"I found out last night."

Mom collapsed on the bed next to me and took off her earrings. "What has got into him?"

"He has this new friend who I think made him feel bad about his work."

"Your dad has a new friend?" she asked, genuinely surprised.

"He's my friend's father."

"Baruch, you have a friend? That is wonderful news. The best news I could've heard." Mom's momness burst through her wifeness and her jet-laggedness. I blushed.

"I also got a girl's number."

Mom grabbed and held me, rocking me back and forth, kissing my head. "That's my boy. That is my boy. I knew it would happen. I knew you had it in you."

Not exactly knowing what the "it" was that I had in me, I took the praise regardless.

"When do I get to meet this friend of yours?"

"We can have him and his dad over for pizza again. You might like Mr. Singh. Dad sure seems to."

Something flicked across Mom's face like a mixture of a twitch and a shadow. "Great, baby. So you know, Dad and I are going to be fighting for a bit and that's just what moms and dads do when dads do dumb stuff without telling their wives. We're not getting a divorce, none of this is because of you. Moms and dads fight, especially when dads are very very stupid men. But I am so proud. I knew there was nothing wrong with you." She got up and cupped my chin in her hands and gave me a long look and kissed my forehead goodnight.

I tried to sleep, but every time I was close to falling off the edge into unconsciousness, a thought pricked me: what had my mom thought might've been wrong with me?

CHAPTER 21

I CALLED OTTILIE. A man answered. I hung up. I wasn't ready for a man to answer. When you talk to a girl's dad do you have to declare your intentions? Were my intentions honorable? Could intentions ever be honorable when they're made by an adolescent meat sack laced with so many hormones that the FDA would immediately reject it for public consumption?

I was barely ready to talk to a girl. I definitely wasn't ready to talk to a dad.

CHAPTER 22

GARY RODE MY BIKE OVER SUNDAY. He was still a little peeved that I had run out on him Friday night. He'd waited at the Long John Silver's for an hour. We always made that our rally place. That way if you got there first you could get something to eat and hang out without drawing attention.

"I ate like four boats of hush puppies," he said. "The manager kept giving me the stink eye, coming over asking me if I wanted anything else. He was racist, man. I've got like puppy poisoning because of you." He was still riding my bike. He made slow circles around me as he talked.

"My bad. How'd you get home?"

"Tammy Somebody came by in her dad's car and she saw me in the window. She had a bunch of her friends. They all really like fried shrimp."

"So that's who goes to Long John Silver's," I said.

"Buzzed teenage girls in their daddy's cars. They were dirty, like way dirty. Kept making dick-sucking jokes with the shrimp."

"What'd you do?"

"We rode around downtown. Tammy tried to get us into a bar but there were too many of us and the door guy was staring at my headwrap, like I was from another planet or something." He paused. "I made out with Darcy Keefer."

"I thought she was into black guys."

"Guess I'm black enough." Gary stopped the bike and said, "She told me she'd never made it with a Muslim before."

"Did you correct her?"

"Why the hell would I?" He tried to pop a wheelie on my ten speed and failed. "At least I wasn't her first nonwhite guy."

"How far did you get?" I held my hands up and made squishing motions then waggled my eyebrows.

"No. Her curfew was up. We dropped her home first. Geography screwed me on that one." He got off my bike and flipped it upside down. "Your derailleur is off. You have a screwdriver?"

"Garage."

I sat on the cement pad as Gary went through my dad's tools. "My mom's back."

"She bring you anything cool from duty-free?"

"More shirts I'll never wear. For some reason she thinks that what's high fashion in South Korea will work in central Ohio."

"My dad's going to want to meet her."

"She said the same thing about meeting you. She's sleeping now though. Jet lag."

"So your dad is working for my dad now."

"Same company. I don't know what his job is."

"He's an executive assistant." Gary found a screwdriver that fit and gave the derailleur a couple of adjustments. "One guess who that executive is."

"Shit."

"It should be fine," Gary said. "My dad's a piece of shit and he'll eventually get fired but it shouldn't blow back on your dad. It's weird but he's taken a kind of real interest in your dad. I've never seen him do that. He's usually aloof at jobs. He tells his stories about being a helicopter engineer during Nam and everyone figures he's the real deal."

"He was in Nam?"

"No. It's just crap he says. Makes people think he's more American than he is. All mega-crap that most people don't check on until he starts acting weird on the job." Gary flipped my bike over. "Give it a try."

I rode around and shifted gears. Everything slotted perfectly. The action was smooth and exact. I got back to the garage. "How do you know how to do this? Work on bikes and stuff?"

"It's just stuff I've picked up from my dad. We're both good with machines."

"I met a girl," I said.

"Rad."

"At the party. I was watching TV and she came up and sat next to me and started talking."

"She hot?" Gary held his hands out in front of him. Hotness for him was purely a breast concern. Boobs. They just arrive in your life. And no one knows how to deal with them. Girls don't know how to adjust their posture for them; to develop too much too fast seemed to give girls in our town a severe case of scoliosis, their spines twisting forward, making a cave of the shoulders to shelter and hide the new arrivals, these migrants fleeing hormonal over-population, seeking a new and better life. Guys who were already unsure and awkward became more so. We snapped bras, annoyed that our cohorts through elementary school were now keeping secrets from us. They had different underwear. They had coin-operated dispensers in their bathrooms. And metal boxes on the walls in their stalls. They seemed in charge of a magic, a language, a cabal for which dudes hadn't even been considered for membership. As boys, going into a girl's restroom was like seeing behind the curtain in *The Wizard of Oz*. There was all of this machinery we didn't know about.

"Oh yeah," I said. But I couldn't remember her boobs, just the way her sentences fell together like she was building houses of cards right in front of you and how they all fell apart almost always. I knew enough not to say this in front of Gary. "Really hot."

"What's her name?"

"She goes to Olentangy. Her name is Ottilie."

"You're going out with a black girl?"

"I think she's half black."

"That's black. In America, that's black." Gary smiled and punched me in the shoulder. "Good boy, Barry. I'm proud of you."

"I just have her number."

"Can I get a glass of water or a pop before I go home?"

"You going to walk?"

"You got a better idea?"

"We'll double on the bike," I said, not knowing how that worked but that people did it. We went inside and filled some glasses with water.

"Can I see those shirts your mom brought you?"

"The crazy Korean ones?"

"Can I borrow a couple of them?"

"You can have them. They're too weird for me. You know they're fucked up, right? Like kind of fancy-boy punk stuff." One of the shirts was torn down the side and held together by a thousand or so safety pins.

"It'd be funny to wear them. Like freak people out a little."

I grabbed a folded grocery bag from the side of the refrigerator. "They are yours. If your ass gets beat, I'm not legally responsible."

Gary was bigger than me but the shirts fit him probably because my mom always bought things for me to grow into. Bad logic when you're buying current fashion. It guarantees that once it fits it'll be out of style. It was punk rock *Miami Vice* Michael Jackson thrown together and pickled like kimchi. Pastel anarchy signs on a shirt with lots of metal studs and zippers that connected nothing to nothing. Gary was ecstatic.

"Are these, y'know, kosher for you to be wearing?" I asked. "As a Sikh and all."

"Sikhism doesn't stop you from being a badass, Barry." He held up one of the shirts to his chest and mugged like a rocker.

My mom with her eye mask still around her neck stumbled into the kitchen. "Morning," she said. Or it sounded like that was what she said. Jet lag hit Mom harder than other people; also she was up all night arguing with Dad.

"This is my friend, Gurbaksh," I said, waving my hands in front of him like he was a show dog.

"Everyone here calls me Gary." He shook my mother's hand before she had steadied herself enough to know he was in the room.

Mom focused on Gary and something happened. She was startled like she'd seen a murder happening across the street. But only for a half second. Like I saw it but I think it was only because I'm her son and her range of looks are all collated and filed away. Here was a look I didn't recognize and I wasn't even sure it really happened because Mom had herself all tucked in now and was chatting with Gary as if nothing had happened.

"How long have you been in town?" she asked.

"Two months now. It's just my father and me. Bachelors, y'know."

"Where do you live?"

"Just over on the other side of the little valley. We can see your bug zapper from our porch."

"We don't have a bug zapper," I said. "Our neighbors do."

"We can see your neighbor's house then," Gary said.

"And how has being a Sikh in our community been?" my mom

asked. "I mean, in our little town it must be difficult. The people here haven't seen all that much beyond the cornfields."

"Gurbaksh is like the most popular kid in school," I said. "People love his turban."

"And your father?" she asked. "How is he finding it? Our town? Professionally? Socially?"

"My father is fine. He likes his job as much as he's ever liked a job. He's a puzzle guy, so when he's given a new puzzle he's happiest." Gary put his hand behind him and grabbed his ankle, stretching his thighs. "He doesn't socialize too much. His best friend is probably your husband."

My mom grimaced. The tiredness was rushing back over her. I figured it'd be best to get Gary out of there before she passed out onto the kitchen floor. I jerked my head at Gary. He got it right away.

"It was nice meeting you, Mrs. Nadler," Gary said. He took her hand and gave it three quick pumps. "Thank you for having me in your home."

We ran out of the kitchen, leaving mom to fight off her jet lag.

I rode him home with him on the handlebars and the whole time he was beaming. It was hard not to be jealous. I kind of didn't want to let the shirts go now. It was hard work pushing us both up the hill towards his home. I zigzagged a lot into the road. People honked at us. Gary waved as they sped past. It was like he was in a parade.

CHAPTER 23

My mom being home was one big argument.

My dad had given up.

My dad had faced reality.

My dad was a coward.

My mom was overreacting.

My mom should have been consulted.

Philosophy didn't count when Reagan was in office.

They were partners and they made decisions together.

My mom was gone all of the time, she was, at best, a silent partner.

My dad had dragged my mom from state to state for years. He was giving up now?

My mom was a pen pal parent, she did cameos as a member of our family.

My dad was throwing away everything he worked for.

My dad was sick of being the weak sister in the house. Nothing was trickling down. Things should be trickling down.

My mom hated all of the travel, hated it, but she did it so he could pursue his dream.

My dad said there came a time to be a man and own up to your responsibilities.

This was West Virginia all over again, wasn't it? This was Arizona all over again?

And they stopped after that one. I could hear them panting, like together they'd just broken the seal off of something huge and were waiting to see what emerged. It was scary in those moments. There was so much of my parents' marriage that I knew nothing about. I felt ill-prepared to take sides.

What emerged was three days of not talking. In some ways, it wasn't quieter. Their silence was the noisiest thing. I was always tripping over it.

CHAPTER 24

DAD'S NEW JOB made more money and the money tore through the house like a tornado. The queer fighting silence between my mom and dad he filled with expensive nonsense.

I had new shoes. A box showed up with all-brass pots and pans. All of the inhabitants of our hodgepodge dish drawer went into the trash. New silverware that all matched. New glassware. All of our Burger King glasses got tossed. We got a dishwasher. I was given a full palette of polo shirts. There was a new sofa. New sheets for every bed. My dad had a sunroof installed in our Corolla. We got a new record player, speakers, radio tuner, and CD player. We had no CDs, but we had a player. There was a VHS player, a laserdisc player, and a membership to Rutherford Audio & Video (RAV's) video rental place, with laminated cards for each member of the family (my mom's sat unclaimed on the kitchen counter). There was a new shower nozzle with five different settings. Dad started drinking Johnny Walker Red. There was new carpet in the living room and a built-in wine rack in the dining room that stretched from floor to ceiling. Mom ignored the new additions and drank her wine out of a box.

The biggest addition was the satellite dish. Dad had ordered it from Sharper Image. It was near one-story high and beige and just like that we went from being a house without a TV to a house with TVs, upstairs and downstairs, and a ton of stolen channels that none of us knew what to do with. Dad watched the TV all the time.

The door to his study now was left open. The chalkboard with a sentence half-diagrammed sat unused, the sentence stuck in its half-deciphered state. It was like a car with its engine parts strewn on the garage floor, not able to run, not clear how to put it back together. Dad was no longer spending his time sequestered in the study. His presence was now everywhere in the house. It was like he was just recognizing that he owned more than the one room. He sat in his leather recliner, remote clenched, a Rusty Nail in a specially ordered drink holder affixed to his recliner (where he found the recipe to this cocktail, I have no idea, but somehow the cocktail made scotch smell worse than it already did). Most nights he slept in the chair. I'd wake him up by turning the TV off.

I didn't know what to think about this new Dad. It didn't seem tenable for him to stay this way. Perhaps he was in some kind of pupa phase. The recliner his cocoon. His imago? No one could know. Here was someone whose intelligence had cordoned him off from the world for most of his life. At best he was a party favor for accountants, dentists, tool & die engineers. And now he was dug tick-deep into the mall culture of middle-manager semi-achievement. Who was he going to be next? Because he couldn't stay this guy for much longer. He had been too smart for this to be the finished Dad product. He was playing hooky from himself.

Mom slept upstairs alone. She quietly postponed a few of her trips.

Dad wanted to throw a party. He told Mom not to worry, he'd have it catered by the grocery store. Mom didn't seem to care if she was invited.

CHAPTER 25

WE WALKED THE FOUR BLOCKS. And stood in front of an old building.

"This is it," Mr. Tyler said.

We couldn't go in. The place hadn't been taken care of. It was built so close to the road it seemed likely to lean on us for support. Mr. Tyler wanted us to really look at it, to really appreciate what history meant.

This is where Rutherford B. Hayes was born. Mr. Tyler wanted us to stand out in the early November cold and appreciate history because he hadn't written a lesson plan beyond the walk down here and back and we'd walked faster than he had estimated and had caught both stoplights.

Gary was shivering. He was wearing the punk rock safety-pin t-shirt and a pale blue patka. He rarely wore the full turban anymore. This patka was cooler. It was like a neat little headband with a topknot.

"Your dad's having a party," he said.

"It's full-on obnoxious."

"You should invite Ottilie, man."

"It's going to be a total bore. My dad will explain what all the remote controls do on the new TV and my mom will get drunk."

"Exactly," he said. He was hunched over, the wind disregarding entirely what he called a shirt. I had a new windbreaker and tried to position myself so that it'd break the wind for both of us. I know how that sounds. I'm not the person who named a piece of clothing after a fart. "You want it to be boring. That way you and I and Ottilie can sneak away from the party, grab a bottle of something, and head upstairs."

"It'll be a threesome?"

Gary spit on the ground. It was an anemic spit. The poor guy's lymph system was joining the fight, trying to keep rail-thin Gary warm. Gary said that in India he'd be called lion-waisted. He was five-seven and his 24"-waist pants would hang off of him no matter how tightly he pulled his braided leather belt. His shoulders were broad and while his hip bones seemed regular-sized, his waist was wrist-sized. His dad had a belly on him, so it was only a matter of time before Gary ballooned out. Now though, shivering in his punk rock t-shirt he looked like a speed freak. "Nah, man. Look, we'll all hang out and then when you feel like the mood is right, you say whip-poor-will and I'll leave you two alone and you can make your move."

"I won't remember that. It's too weird of a word."

"It's supposed to be. That way you won't accidentally say it when it's not time."

"How about cardinal?" I asked. "It is the state bird."

"Whatever, you freak. Just say it and I'll take off."

Mr. Tyler sauntered over to us and we shut up and started soaking in the history. The building was old. It was wood. It was brown. It'd fall down if someone didn't pony up some dough soon. And who would want to donate enough money to commemorate Rutherford B. Hayes? He didn't even win the election. Samuel Tilden, the democrat from New York, did. The conservatives were too freaked out by Tilden's reputation as a reformer, and with the state of the union being still precarious in 1876, the smoky backroom of American politics got Florida to fake enough votes so its electoral total went Hayes's way. What did Hayes have to teach us really? To be quiet and unobtrusive enough so that you'd be a suitable candidate when the real powers-that-be wanted someone easy to manipulate. None of this we went over in class. He was local pride. A two-headed calf would deserve as much historical attention. And we stood outside of where his mother birthed him and we all shivered in the central Ohio November wind trying to figure out how to elevate a dilapidated old house to historical importance. The only thing Hayes had to teach us was that if we wanted to do anything in our lives, we needed to get out and never look back.

Fuck Rutherford.

"Boys," Mr. Tyler said behind us. "You getting this?"

"Yessir," we both mumbled.

"We're sending teachers to space, Halley's Comet is coming back, there's the gay plague, and a woman was a vice-presidential candidate of a 'major' party." You could hear the air-quotes Mr. Tyler put around "major." Democrats weren't anything but a major pain in his ass, but it was swell of the sure-losers to put up a lady. Reagan seemed to make men think all men thought the same. "The world is changing right before our eyes, boys. Good or bad. You can't even imagine what the future has in store."

"Is that why you teach history?" I asked, trying to make Gary laugh. "Cause you've got no idea about the future?"

"Shut up, Yo-Yo Faggot," Mr. Tyler said and walked away.

CHAPTER 26

MY FACE WAS HOT all day after that. I couldn't even get my head around the fact that he had said it at all. The panic stuff was on me but set on simmer. My esophagus wanted nothing to do with my body anymore. It strained at my throat, felt like it was trying to tear free, but not so much that I could plausibly go to the nurse. What would I tell her if I went? A teacher called me something bad and now my breathing tube was getting shoehorned out of my body? You go in for symptoms like that and you get sent to a guidance counselor and I couldn't risk another meltdown. Now that my dad wasn't a professor, I didn't want to screw up my college chances totally by being me. Maybe no one else noticed it happened. Maybe it hadn't happened at all. Maybe I was called it so often by my peers that I just misheard Mr. Tyler.

On the bus, Gary sat next to me.

"Holy fuck, are you okay?" he asked.

"I'm fine," I lied.

"That was so fucked up. A teacher, man. A teacher called you that. You're certified now."

"I don't think anyone else heard it," I said. I pulled my backpack up from the floor and looked through it for, I don't know, a wormhole out of this dimension.

"Everyone heard it, man."

"Not everyone."

"Every. Fucking. One. Heard it," he said, slapping the syllables out on the green vinyl seat. "It's all over the school."

"Did you tell anyone?"

"No," he said. "I mean, yes. How could I not? Mr. Tyler is an asshole. This should get him fired."

"I don't think it was that bad."

"He called you a faggot in front of the whole class." Gary's eyes were bugging out of his skull. "Don't you see that he's over? Don't you know what he's done to you? You know it's fucked up, right?"

"Students call me that all the time."

"Yeah, but a teacher? That's a line, man. A line that shouldn't be crossed."

"Probably heard it from his wrestlers," I said. The panic simmer was turning to a rolling boil. My rib cage started to feel like it was shrinking.

"Doesn't matter where he heard it. He shouldn't have said it. I'm serious, we could get him fired because of this."

I watched out the window. I wanted to find something I could focus on, freeze it in my mind, and trade places with it. There was a hydrant. Would I rather be a hydrant than me? Yeah. "You're making too big a deal out of this."

"You might have to change schools."

"He called me 'Yo-Yo Faggot,'" I said. "He didn't even get it right."

"Does that matter?"

"I mean there's a difference between fag and faggot, right?"

Gary stared at me in disbelief. "Like one's the formal address? Since he called you 'faggot' he was showing you more respect?"

"Right. It's like the difference between 'gaylord' and 'gaywad.'"

Gary laughed. "There's a difference?"

"A gaylord is part of the landed gentry," I said. "He's got serfs and shit. A gaywad is . . . something else."

"Gay serfs."

"Serfs nonetheless."

Gary was doubled over. "You're fucked up, Barry." A beat passed and Gary said, "Really, though, if we're not going to get him fired what are we going to do?"

"Like what?"

"Like payback, man. Like totally mess him up."

"I'm not," I said, my mind wheeling at the possibility of retribution. "I don't know if that's my thing."

"We look in the phone book, find his address, and go over to his house in the middle of the night."

"And what? Key his car? Toilet paper his house?"

"At least. That's the right direction. Do some kind of lasting shit to him."

The bus stopped. The redheaded girl got off. Porky Boxwell and Holly Trowbridge walked by hand in hand. They passed by in silence. Their silence was awful. It was better when they'd just make fun of me.

Gary paused and made sure he had eye contact with me. He was starting to let his beard grow. There were soft little whiskers littering his face. Less like a beard and more like hair acne. "What if you could do anything to him? Like fuck him up for good."

"Like I was all-powerful and no one would ever find out? I'd do that thing Bill Murray talks about in *Caddyshack*. Slice his Achilles tendon as he pulls back for his golf swing."

"Yeah." Gary slapped the back of the seat. "That's what I'm talking about."

"I'd lead him into a factory and have him chase me through a stamping machine and turn it on right when he was in the middle of it."

"Splat! Eyeballs and shit everywhere."

"Language," the bus lady said.

"He could jump on me and I'd throw him in the microwave and turn it on."

"There are people-sized microwaves?"

"It's from *Gremlins*," I said.

"Oh. I don't see many movies."

"Then I could go all Kali Ma and tear his heart out from his chest."

"Jesus, dude. That's dark."

"It's Indiana Jones. You really don't see any movies, do you?"

"My dad says they're all racist. The Hollywood ones."

"They probably are."

"Also there's no singing or dancing like Bollywood ones so he thinks they're a rip-off."

We sat there as Rutherford rolled by our pinch-and-pull-down windows. Race never really came up between Gary and me. But when it did, it was like we were sitting in a really bad fart and didn't want to acknowledge it. The thing was that I envied Gary. I envied his turban. I envied his brownness. I figured it was his brownness, his turban, that allowed him to be so popular. He stood out. But not in the way that I stood out: my weakness on display for everyone. People just naturally avoided and despised me like a Band-Aid in the pool. I liked being friends with Gary, I liked being around his brownness, I liked that his brownness was now associated with me. But we didn't talk about his brownness. I researched him. I read about Sikhism as fast as interlibrary loan would allow. I figured I would know him then, decode his affect, distill and bottle his personality. What does anyone want in a best friend other than to swallow him up and own what makes him different from you? Is this so different because he's brown? Would I research a white friend if I had one?

I was getting a headache. The same kind I got when Dad used to explain Hegel to me. Sometimes you stand at the edge of what you know and you can see spread out in front of you all that you don't.

But it's smeared in fog. There were times when I learned something I could feel it, like could feel it altering my brain—and I knew the cliff had extended a little bit further out into the fog.

Example: the movie *Alien*—at first I thought space suits were like scuba-diving suits. But the ocean is full of life, just not hospitable to us. Space is so enormous and made up of so much nothing that when the crew woke up from their pods suddenly I felt small and I could feel my brain adjust to this new reality. We're tiny and insignificant from the point of view of space. The moon doesn't care if we visit it. Space doesn't care that we're sending up a teacher in January. Space doesn't care about us. It doesn't even have the capacity to be indifferent. Like language is impossible as a means to describe space. It's a negation. It's not.

Is this how Gary felt? A not? The Jewish kids were different but they blended in and most of the school was too dumb to know what Jewish meant. But the school knew what "brown" meant and had an idea of what "turban" meant. But Gary disarmed all of that. People loved Gary. Teachers, lunch ladies, students, custodians, all fell under his spell. But was this the result of having lived as a "not" for so long? Was he constantly his own PR agency?

The black kids, after about sixth grade, started to hang out exclusively with one another. Maybe fifth grade had become the year they'd started having to be their own PR agencies and maybe sixth was when they decided to close up shop.

Was Gary so nice, funny, smart, and outgoing because if he wasn't something bad would happen? Did he know something about us, small-town Ohio, that we didn't know about ourselves? I could feel the locks and slides moving in my brain trying to accept this new kind of thinking.

My stop was here. Gary was already standing in the aisle to let me pass.

"Monsignor Yo-Yo Faggot, I believe this is your stop," he said, bowing.

"See you tonight," I said.

"Wouldn't miss it," he said. "Actually not allowed to miss it. Papa Singh is a little too excited about this party."

CHAPTER 27

MY MOM HAS ALWAYS worried about my popularity.

She had been in the Homecoming Court three times and thinks it meant something. And maybe it does. Maybe it's where she gets her fearlessness from: those days sitting on floats riding through town waving at strangers might have been the perfect training for a job in hotel development. But it's not for me. Not that I choose to not be popular as an ascetic choice—it's not in the cards for a short skinny weenie who can now officially go an entire week wearing different Batman-themed shirts. I've never had the heart to break it to my mom what they call me at school.

My mom is undeterred. She wants me to let her take me to a stylist to do my hair, instead of the five-dollar barber cuts I've been getting for years. She tells me that these are the best years of my life. She doesn't know how much that depresses me.

CHAPTER 28

I DIALED OTTILIE'S NUMBER again at five. It rang three times. She answered this time.

"Hey, have you been calling and hanging up a lot?"

"No. I don't think so."

"You don't think so? My dad's pissed. He's worried there's something wrong with our line. He's going to have the phone company come out and check it. It's like three hundred dollars for a service visit and line check."

There was a long pause.

"It was me," I said.

"Hah! I knew it, you stalker." She was laughing. I wanted to like her laughter more than feeling humiliated, but it wasn't going to happen. "Did my dad scare you? He's got that voice."

"It's deep," I said.

"He only does it when he answers the phone. My mom is allergic to dogs so he's like, 'Somebody has to guard this place.' Personally, I think he thinks he's not black enough because he bought a Phil Collins record and likes jigsaw puzzles, so he does the phone voice to compensate. He's the nerdiest guy in real life. He's a chemist."

"Your mom is white, right?"

"Swedish. He couldn't have married a whiter woman."

There was a pause again. How did people do this? Talking to girls was fine when they were speaking but in the gaps between it was awful.

"You were lying about the phone company," I said.

She laughed. "You're not my first pervert. I was totally going to hang up on you if you didn't own up to it."

"You just tested me."

"And you passed! Doesn't that feel good? You passed. And your reward is that you get to keep talking to me, which is way more valuable than you might think."

"You've had perverts?"

"Yeah. Just one but I'm young still. He came to the house a lot to do homework with me and then I started to notice that my underwear was going missing, which is so gross to think of the kid I did differential equations with jerking himself off with my underwear. When I figured out what he was doing, I told my parents and they called the cops on him. It was so embarrassing. Like we ended up going over to his house with the police to tell his parents what he was doing, so they could like send him to counseling or whatever. They thought I wanted my underwear back and while we sat there in their dining room sent him to put them all in a paper bag to give back to me."

"That's gross," I said, and remembered not to tell her that I was supposed to be in counseling myself.

"Right? Like I'd ever want them back. They just sat there on the dining room table in the paper bag while the adults and the police officer talked it all out. We were going to have a restraining order put on him, which is super rare for a minor to get, like no kid gets a restraining order, right? But he switched schools instead, which is kind of unfair because it's like he gets a blank slate somewhere new and he'll end up doing it to some other girl. I don't know which school he transferred to. Do you know how to find stuff like that out?"

Pause again. Did I know?

"I don't think so. Unless you called every school in the phone book asking if he's there, enrolled or whatever." I was cobbling sentences together. It was taking effort to answer her. She talked in streams of information while I had to hand-build my sentences.

"I think people, like the girls at his new school, should know what kind of pervert is around them. It's like their right to know. Right? Like he should wear something like Hester Prynne had to. Except Hester wasn't really guilty of anything other than banging the hot preacher."

"At least you got all-new underwear out of it."

"No. I just have to wear all the gross ones he wouldn't steal."

There was a large pause.

"You're thinking about my bottom," she sang into the phone. "You're totally a perv too. God, I'm like a perv magnet."

"I'm not. I'm not a pervert. I swear. I wouldn't even know how to begin."

"Begin what?"

"I don't know. I'm flummoxed." My chest was tightening. I could feel the air getting thicker in my lungs. I pinched my thigh as hard as I could.

"Flummoxed. Good vocab word, perv."

"Can we stop talking about your underwear?"

"I think it'd be best. Oh my God, I can't believe I just told you that whole thing. It was a mess and traumatized me like crazy and now I'm just telling strangers about it like it was just a weird thing that happened. I'm totally messed up."

"Do you want to come to a party?"

"I don't know. I'm not really a party person. Isn't that like how we met? By us both not being party people? Weren't we hiding from a party the last time? Are you really asking me to hide from a party with you?"

"Yes. It's a party my dad is throwing."

"Do you have brothers and sisters?"

"I'm an only."

"So you and I will be the only kids at the party?"

"My friend Gary is coming too."

"Gary was at that other party, where we met. That Gary? With the turban? The Muslim guy? He's a friend of yours?"

"He's my best friend. He's a Sikh, not a Muslim."

"Whatever. He's really loud and obnoxious. At least he was the night of the party."

"He's my best friend and really nice. One of the smartest people I know."

"I'm the smartest person you know."

"You think Dimmesdale is hot."

"So?"

"I don't think there's textual evidence backing up your claim."

"When's this party you want me to avoid with you and this best friend and second-smartest person you know, Gary?"

"Tonight," I said.

"Not a lot of warning."

"Yeah, I tried calling earlier but your dad kept answering."

"What makes you think I'd be free? It's a Friday night. I could have plans. Movies. Boyfriends. Sleepovers. Football games. Parties where the parents aren't home. Smoking weed and listening to Pink Floyd in somebody's basement."

"Do you have a boyfriend?"

"I barely have friends, perv."

"You'll come?"

"Sure. Why not?"

"Great. I'll go to the library and pick up a concordance of *The Scarlet Letter* for you. Because nowhere does it say that Dimmesdale is Tom Cruise–esque."

"Now you're just showing off."

My chest released a little. The air was less viscous as it moved in and out of me. I was talking to a girl on the phone. It wasn't that hard either. There was a rhythm to it. I'd found the rhythm. I was so relieved at being relieved that I forgot I was on the phone.

"Are you going to give me the address?"

"Right. Of course."

"And what's this party for anyway? What am I walking into?"

"It's a party my dad is throwing because he isn't teaching philosophy anymore."

"I have absolutely no idea what to wear to such a thing."

"Yeah. Nobody does."

There was silence on the line. I tried to hear the room she was in. I wanted to hear around her breathing to the sounds of her house. What did a room that held her feel like? What sounds did it make in response to housing someone like her? I felt dirty doing it. Like I was some kind of ear-peeking weirdo. Was ear-peeking even a thing?

"I'll just wear a prom dress unless you have further instructions," she said.

Eavesdropping. Eavesdropping was the name for ear-peeking. I am a total jerk-off moron.

"Prom dress sounds great. I'll wear one too."

But that's not true. Eavesdropping was when you listened to someone else's conversation. I just wanted to listen to her house. The ambient stuff around her. The floor creaking under her weight, the microwave beeping, the cabinets clapping shut, the scraping that could be a dog at the door or a storm outside pushing branches against her window. I was breaking into her house with my left ear.

"Are you going to hold me hostage like this forever or are you going to tell me where you live?" she asked.

CHAPTER 29

Why do parents invite their children to their parties?

The kids don't want to be there, feeling more like show ponies than anything else. "Marvin excels in Latin. Speak Latin, Marvin."

And the parents don't get to act like they want to because the kids are around. We become the moral governors on the engines of our parents' hedonism.

I worked on that sentence for a while. I want to say it to Ottilie at the party. That sentence is as much about getting ready for the night as picking out the shirt that Tammy Barker, a cheerleader, told me was cute, as much as making sure I had clean underwear, or arranging the magazines my dad started subscribing to in a fan display on the coffee table.

We never used to have magazines. We had journals: the design-impoverished philosophy periodicals that had fifty-page articles about Plato's use of articles. If hurled with the right force, they were thick enough to break the spine of a possum. Now all of those journals were tossed. And now we had *Utne Reader, Reason, Ms.* magazine, *The Nation,* and *The New Yorker.* They were the kind of subscriptions that probably had us on some FBI anti-Communist watch list. The only one I read was *Ms.* I was at first totally mystified about what I found in it. And then I kept reading hoping that I'd figure women out once and for all, like maybe I just needed to quote Andrea Dworkin to break the ice with cheerleaders, let them know I was down with their struggle. There was an interview with a novelist named Kathy Acker in which she stated that she'd written her last novel "with a dildo in her cunt" the entire time. This left me very confused about the writing process.

My dad was downstairs peeling the plastic off of the trays of shrimp and the six-foot hoagie he bought special from the deli.

When I went downstairs, my parents were arguing about it.

"Why did you put the sandwich on different plates?" he asked.

"People need to talk," Mom said. "It's intimate this way."

"But why buy a six-foot sub if you're just going to slice it up. People need to see it as an enormous sub."

Dad started grabbing all of the sandwich slices off of the pinwheel plates and tried reassembling them.

"You have no sense of presentation."

"Clearly, you're the one who's devoid of panache."

"This is panache?" Mom gestured to the misshapen monster sandwich Dad was trying to reassemble. "My way people can have their own conversations."

Dad ignored her. "This is spectacle. Grandeur. The fatted calf has been slaughtered."

"It's another blackboard. You've always got to have your blackboard, don't you, Professor." Mom poured herself a drink and lit a cigarette. "What lecture are we in for this evening?"

"Can you be happy for me for one night?"

"The man I love has given up his dream. Let's party."

"Giving up a dream. That means waking up. I've woken up. Your husband has woken up and is finally joining the world."

"Hence that." Mom pointed at the sandwich, which now resembled a kind of slapdash horror-show deli abattoir. We all paused and looked at it. Mushed bread and herniated toppings, with circles of meat hanging out like tongues. "Good morning," she said and left the room.

This was a pet theory of Mom's: most people who teach at the college level have some level of social awkwardness. Lectures are a way out of that. The teacher gets to stand in front of everyone and say exactly what he has already written down, something he's probably said about a hundred times before. Every class is a rehearsal for them and maybe someday they'll get it right and be able to talk like a normal person.

My dad was far from this goal. You could see him trying to picture group conversations as seminars. He didn't participate, he moderated. Sometimes people felt sorry for him.

I took the garbage out, I put an extra roll of toilet paper on the tank of the toilet, I stayed busy and out of range of the battle. My parents would have to put the knives away before guests arrived but until then they'd each try to draw as much blood as they could. Then they'd each have a drink. They'd be exsanguinated and flushed as they took coats, shook hands, and pointed the way to the makeshift bar. Hopefully by the time the guests arrived Mom would be drunk enough so that she'd have gained some perspective (it was Dad's party after all), but not so loud that she'd have lost discretion. I'd seen their fights. I didn't want Ottilie or Gary seeing their fights.

Mom was good at talking at parties. She did this thing where she talked just a half-decibel too quietly and anyone she was talking to would have to lean in to hear her better. This was all affectation. She was equally proud of her perfume and her cleavage. And this way people got a double dose of it.

When is childhood over? Maybe it's when you see your mom use her tits to get things she wanted.

What's maddening about this is that my mother was brilliant and mega-business savvy. It was almost as if these gestures were a kind of survivor's guilt for being a successful woman in business. A way of her saying, "Yes, you're probably right. I'm only this successful because I've flirted and shaken my goods all the way to upper-management." She wouldn't allow herself to actually acknowledge how great her accomplishments were so she bought push-up bras from Frederick's of Hollywood and practically bathed in duty-free perfume.

Dad knew this about her and went out of his way as a courtesy to never slip up and give her a compliment.

When is childhood over? When you realize which of the sado-masochistic roles your parents play in their relationship.

The party was to begin at 7:00 but no one ever arrived before 7:15 to any party ever. Not so much to be fashionably late (that was a Columbus or Cincinnati affectation) or due to traffic (there was none), but because no one wanted to be impolite enough to be the first ones to arrive. So when the doorbell rang at 6:45 we all froze.

Dad's shirt wasn't tucked in, Mom still had to put her face on. When you're an only child you're the one who does what no one else wants to. I went and answered the door.

At the door weren't guests, but delivery men carrying flowers.

When I opened the door to tell them they had the wrong address it was like I had broken open a flower piñata. At least seven men all in striped short-sleeved shirts bearing the FTD logo: Mercury in his tin hat and lightning-bolt feet carrying a bouquet. The men were armed with all kinds of flowers and set to populating every flat surface with them. And when the vases and armloads of arrangements had been set down, the men streamed out to their three trucks to carry more in. A palette of rose varieties bunched conspicuously casually in paper-thin glass vases, chrysanthemums in stout mugs, calla lilies bending their necks down from their bulbous containers, birds of paradise and an orchid or three in dirt and wire, sunflowers rubber-banded together at the stalk, acres of daisies, violets, some blue numbers that looked like little fairy fists raised in the air like they were at a rally, asters, delphinium, hydrangea, eryngium, decorative moss, a bonsai or two—the whole genus came and overwhelmed our living room, kitchen, and dining rooms—not so much a curated selection of flowers as a "whatever you got" order. After twenty minutes of the men practically forming a fireman's line from their trucks to our house and a stunned signature coaxed from my father, our house had been transformed into a greenhouse, a three-bedroom two-bath Eden, a late nineteenth-century farmhouse designed by Kublai Khan. The poor six-foot hoagie looked all the worse in this new setting. Its little plastic squeeze bottles of oil and vinegar hid in the fist-sized carnations—at least they had the decency to know they were outclassed.

The note that came with the flowers didn't help at all to explain their appearance: "One less thing for Mrs. Callaway to attend to herself."

My dad read it three times aloud and turned it over several times looking for a signature that wasn't there. He called the leader of the florists—the bloom overseer, the prince of the pansies—over to haggle out the clear mistake. "No one here is named Callaway." The herald of the hydrangeas pointed out the time, location, and date of the delivery. There had been considerable coordination as the greenhouses as far as Worthington and Lancaster had been emptied for this display.

"Lancaster?" my father asked, as if this was the final absurdity he would no longer stand for. The flower guys, the garland gang, the posy posse finally felt the work had been completed and began their departure. Mother was staring at the card that came with the flowers when another truck pulled up. This time it was fruit. Oranges and apples and watermelons and kiwis. The exact same card as the last one. Unsigned. "One less thing for Mrs. Callaway to attend to herself." Mom snatched that one from my hand before she ran upstairs.

There was a deli truck. Trays of meat arrayed on plastic plates. Olives stuffed with almonds. Cubes of marbled cheese with toothpicks. And then came a liquor truck. Champagne, gin, whiskey, vodka, and a man who installed himself in the corner of our den with the liquor and glassware arranged around him. He didn't speak as he set up. Just stood there in his wedding-DJ attire: jacketless, suspenders, sleeves of his crisp shirt rolled up, his mauve tie tucked in between his third and fourth button. He placed a card on his table.

"My name is Trevor. I can make any cocktail you can dream of. Please try and stump me. *Awarded Best Bartender three years in a row by the* Columbus Dispatch."

Trevor had a curly-haired mullet that touched his shirt collar. Trevor seemed as ready for making drinks as he was for engaging in some martial arts or military drills. The muscles in his forearms were twitching. Trevor didn't seem real so much as a figment of the imagination of a person you never wanted to meet.

And then the sound system arrived. There were cables and generators and an honest-to-God DJ. The best I'd ever experienced at a party was someone who had synced all their tapes up to the best songs and spent the party shuffling them in and out of the two-deck boom box. The two-deck boom box had always seemed so urbane and worldly, capable of so much. The boom box brought the subway with it, brought graffiti with it, brought all of the things assigned as the modern plagues. Sleeveless denim jackets even.

But a real DJ? And it wasn't a fancy relative's wedding? Some real *Max Dugan Returns* shit was going down. There were even lights. With gels and a strobe. People—old people—didn't dance at Ohio parties. The DJ set up on our back deck and within ten minutes was doing a mic check. He played "Almost Paradise" from the *Footloose* soundtrack as mood music for the delivery people still setting up.

My dad was flummoxed. He tried to get Trevor to say who hired him. Who knows how many times Trevor was beaten up in his life? But you could get a ballpark figure from the smug way he enjoyed telling my dad that, "My employment is privileged information. Could I interest you in a gin rickey? I can also do an Ohio variation, the Branch Gin Rickey." He giggled a little as he said it. He fucking giggled.

I wanted to punch the guy and I wasn't the one having a conversation with him. Instead my dad deflated a little and asked for a Rusty Nail.

"One Tetanus coming right up," he said and giggled again.

As if a secret word had been uttered on a frequency my dad and I couldn't hear, all of the delivery people disappeared at once. Should I say "seemed to disappear"? Because it would have been impossible for them all to have such a complicated choreographed exit planned out ahead of time. But they really were all gone almost immediately. Just the DJ, Trevor, and a guy I hadn't seen before in the kitchen with a whole setup consisting of a hot light and a giant slab of prime rib in front of him. He was sharpening his knife as I walked by. There was a tidy stack of white plates next to him. Whatever had to happen to make you not recognize your own house had happened.

Then the guests started to arrive. They walked into the house dazed, like how the dead arriving at the river Lethe must feel. It was too much of a transition. I helped slip their jackets from them. I directed them to Trevor.

The first people to arrive were colleagues—former colleagues—of my dad's from the college and some from over at Ohio Wesleyan, Ohio State. They had come to gloat, to comfort their old boy as he left the world of ideas for the world of commissions and accounts receivable. Their jaws dropped once they entered. Some philosophers believe that there is a place where an experience so unexpected can leave us without language to digest the experience with. It's called aporia, a place without pores, without handholds, without traction for the brain to dig into and continue motoring along its predetermined ruts. Aporias are where we find the limits of ourselves, of what experience has prepared us to expect from the world. We're animals born into language and when language fails, we slip back into animal skittishness. I watched the philosophy department of Rutherford College stumble about on coltish legs in their individual aporias as they took in the flowers, the DJ, the prime rib, Trevor.

Dad was shaking people's hands and pulling them into little half conversations. When I dumped an armload of coats into the office, I heard the shower running. I went upstairs and knocked on the door.

"Mom?"

There was sobbing. The shower was running and my mom was crying.

"Mom?" I knocked again. Quieter this time. Like a confidential knocking. "Mom, the party has started. People are arriving."

Our house has transoms in the upstairs rooms. The glass in the bathroom one was painted but it was always left open. Steam coursed through it.

"Tell them to go away. Cancel it all," my mom said as she cried. "Bring me a drink," she added and laughed a little.

"What's going on, Mom?"

She laughed again and opened the door. She was fully dressed and had been standing under the shower. "I've done something awful," she said.

"It's not that bad. You just took a shower with your clothes on," I said. And she hugged me tight. We sat on the floor in the bathroom. My mom's hair in a wet web in front of her face. Her dress made squishing sounds when she moved. "This is ruined," she said, waggling one of her sleeves. In her hand were the cards from the caterers, the florists, Trevor, all waterlogged and disintegrating. "I'm not very good at any of this," she said and sagged into me. "Please tell me what I should do, Baruch."

We sat there for a while. I thought about Ottilie arriving at the party and having no one to talk to. I thought about Gurbaksh and his dad. I was going to have to change clothes. My one really good collared shirt was now wet. My mom cried a bit more. She'd turned forty-two in October. I'd forgotten like I always do. I wished I hadn't. Maybe Mom wouldn't be here crying if I had been more attentive. But she was never here. It would've been like celebrating a ghost's birthday.

Eventually I got a towel around her and coaxed her into getting changed. Her wet clothes were a swampy lump on the bathroom floor. The music from downstairs rattled the toothbrushes.

I had nothing clean other than the one South Korean punk shirt I hadn't given to Gurbaksh. I thought it'd be nice if I wore one of them for her. Mom put on a dress I'd rarely seen and heels. She was putting on pantyhose when I walked in to check on her. I knocked, she said come in. And there she was doing this weird deep knee bend squat thing to get the pantyhose on. I turned away. In my stomach I knew that whatever I saw was more intimate than seeing her naked. As we went downstairs together to join the party, I was sad for Mom. I hadn't realized how much she didn't like my dad's new job.

While we had been upstairs, the party had taken a deep breath in and there were adults everywhere. Adults are the oxygen in that metaphor.

Adults with drinks and wet napkins. Adults forcing scraps of food into their mouths. Adults touching a person's shoulder as they laughed. Adults sucking prime rib juice from their fingers. Adults standing in line for the bathroom staring at our wall art. Adults confiding to the next person in line that there wasn't any more toilet paper. Adults grabbing the car keys from their husbands. Adults laughing at unfunny jokes. Adults discussing politics. Adults pouting.

Adults staring a moment too long at somebody's chest. Adults being bad sports. Adults spilling their drinks on someone. Adults laughing at being spilled on. Adults looking for towels. Adults getting more drinks. Adults standing in a circle, listening to the music. Adults sitting on the lawn. Adults leaning in for a light. Adults putting their arms around each other. Adults taking off their blazers. Adults examining the satellite dish. Adults parking each other in. Adults slamming car doors in the darkness. Adults not ringing the doorbell. Adults coming right in. Adults crossing their legs. Adults knocking the magazines to the floor with their feet. Adults watching TV. Adults stuffing assorted nuts into their faces. Adults introducing themselves. Adults asking each other how they know my parents. Adults piling their coats on a bed in the guest room. Adults stacking meat and cheese cubes on a cracker. Adults stuffing it all in their mouth. Adults coughing. Little flecks of food coming out of adult mouths. Adults asking to use the phone. Adults assuring the room that it wasn't long distance. Adults agreeing with Reagan. Adults hating Reagan. Adults trying to keep it polite. Adults wishing they hadn't worn a sweater. Adults loosening their ties. Adults who didn't know anyone here. Adults telling their spouses that they couldn't go home yet, it was all just getting started.

My dad invited some of his old students to the party. They brought their friends. And when they saw the free booze, they called their friends. Soon the party was over a hundred people. The students wore jam shorts and half shirts and spaghetti-strapped jersey knit dresses. The students shouted eight different drink orders at Trevor and then dropped at least two of them as they moved back to their friends. The students bummed cigarettes and crowded the dance floor.

The DJ played "Shout." The DJ played "Louie, Louie." He played "Hang On, Sloopy" and "Respect." Dance music having stalled out in Central Ohio at the *Animal House* soundtrack. The DJ said he was going to bring things down a little and the dance floor/back deck emptied while he played "My Girl." Three couples clutched each other and danced. Two male students did a jokey swing dance thing, theatrically grabbing each other's butts. Adults laughed.

I got my mom a glass of wine and deposited her on the couch. She smoothed her dress with the flat of her hand.

"You're a good boy, Baruch. Better than I've ever deserved," she whispered in my ear.

I nodded. I never liked how sincere she could get. It made me feel small. It made me realize I could never be that uncomplicatedly sincere with her about my emotions towards her.

I saw Gurbaksh sitting on the piano bench. Next to him was Ottilie. They were pushing the keys on the piano and laughing. The party was so loud I couldn't hear what they were playing. The only teenagers here. The only brown people here. Their age and their skin probably enacted a kind of gravity on each other. Of course, in all of these people they'd find each other.

The crowd was impossibly thick. I pushed my way through it slowly over to them. I looked back at my mom and saw Mr. Singh float over to her. His red turban hovered above the crowd like a body-surfing ladybug. He gave a little bow and my mom put her hands to her mouth and then she shook her head violently. She was crying. A woman with a cigarette tottering backward on her heels swung her hand to try and find balance, crushing the cherry of her cigarette into my bicep. I yelped. No one noticed. The woman laughed to the men she was talking to, shoved the cigarette back in her mouth, and brushed something off of her dress. The pain seared through me. The crowd swallowed me up. It was a forest of tweed and nylon. I wanted to flop to my stomach and worm my way through on my belly.

I said "excuse me" to no one in particular and pushed my way through.

"You guys met?" I asked.

They looked up from the piano as if I'd caught them doing something.

"Holy shit, man. There you are," Gurbaksh said. He jumped up from the piano bench and pushed me down on it. "This is so weird."

"Like this is crazy. The entire lawn is full of cars. I didn't know there were this many people in town," Ottilie said.

I noticed immediately how she didn't say hi to me. I was swallowed into their conversation. The pain in my arm flared.

"Rutherfuck, Nohio, is on fire tonight," Gurbaksh said.

"Is there some place we can escape to? We didn't want to explore too much without you," she said.

"There's the garage. It's an old barn, really," I said.

"I'll get us drinks," Gurbaksh said and disappeared into the thicket of adults.

Ottilie and I pushed our way out to the backyard and across the crowded driveway. We startled a couple clutching each other in the dark. We were way more embarrassed than they were.

The lights were already on in the barn. An owlish man was standing staring at the walls. He swayed a little as he told us, "This is all original centennial construction. Red Elm." He knocked on the wall, a fine mist of dust sprinkling from the roof. "A horse barn. Maybe some grain storage. Not very much. Just enough for the house to use in the winter. There's probably a missing larder somewhere." The man turned to us, his owl eyes bulging, and solemnly said, "Could you point me in the direction of the root cellar?"

"The basement?" I asked.

"More than likely," he slurred.

"We don't let guests in the basement," I said.

"Oh." He wobbled past the lawnmower and left the barn saying "how rude" under his breath.

Ottilie grabbed the drink the man left behind and swallowed it down in one motion.

"It's like a nature documentary out there," she said.

"I don't know where all those people came from."

"Gurbaksh said his dad catered the whole thing."

"Is that where all of that stuff came from? That solves a big mystery for us. I mean, my dad did some of it," I said, thinking of the sad six-foot sub my dad had thought would be sufficient. "But the DJ and stuff was a total surprise."

"The bartender stared at my chest. He's a total perv."

"Gross," I said, reminding myself to not look at her chest. She was wearing a purple t-shirt with neon turtles on it. She'd cut the crew neck out of it and the shirt hung off her shoulders.

"Nice weird old barn," she said. "Did you bring me out here to kill me? Or do you want to kill me in the root cellar? Bury me in your larder, Baruch."

"I, uh . . ." Nothing came out. I didn't know how to play this game of shocking statements.

"You could totally dismember me and hide it all in the root cellar." Her voice was still as bubbly when it described acts of awful violence.

I tried to come up with something to say and only came up with a million sure-failures. "How's Olentangy?"

She pouted momentarily. "You mean as a school organism?" She hopped up onto the hood of the lawnmower. "I don't know. Boring?"

The air in the barn felt miserable. Too close and stinking of ancient horses. "Do you have a favorite, a favorite subject or activity or something?"

"Jesus, you're worse than my uncles. Can't we talk about something other than school? You've got me alone in your barn. Tell me about your weird shirt. Did you wear that to impress me?"

I'd forgotten my shirt. It was a black tank top that was torn and stitched back together in four jagged seams. It had something scrawled across it in Korean graffiti letters. The shirt was like the cabinet full of miniature bottles of shampoo and soap and conditioner, all the things my mom brought home that were evidence of how much time she spent away. I'd forgotten my mom. Twenty minutes ago I was pulling her crying from a shower. I abandoned her on the sofa at a party she didn't want to have.

"Just something my mom got in Korea. I was wearing something else but it got wet." My arms were cool in the shirt. I never wore tank tops because they showed off my narrow little arms. "I might need to go find my dad."

Ottilie stared at me. Her stare made all the air fall out of the garage. On my tongue, I could feel the little specks of dust the owlish man had let loose. Is this what people meant when they talked about beautiful people? Like if I just stared at her nose I was fine. If I just stared at her left earlobe I was fine. But to look directly at her made something awful happen to my stomach. It was like when I looked right at her I could get a sense of how disappointing I was to her, a scrawny kid in a dumb shirt in a dusty old barn. Beautiful people must always be so disappointed in the world. It must be their defining trait.

Or maybe she just didn't understand why I was going to leave her alone.

"Don't anyone worry. I come bearing refreshments," Gurbaksh shouted as he came in. He was balancing four drinks in his hands. "I didn't know what you guys liked so I grabbed enough for choices. It also made that Trevor guy think I was getting these drinks for adults."

A blond woman followed Gurbaksh into the barn. It took me a second too long to realize that it was Stacey from the restaurant. She had makeup on and was wearing a pastel leotard with a skirt.

"Oh," she said when she saw me. She had three wine coolers in her hands. "I'm not sure I should be giving you these. Gurbaksh made it sound like y'all were college students."

"My dad invited you?"

"Jesus. Rude much?" Ottilie said as she pushed past me and grabbed one of the wine coolers from Stacey's hand.

"Are we interrupting anything?" Gurbaksh waggled his eyebrows at me.

"Baruch was just leaving."

Everyone looked at me.

"I was just going to find my dad and tell him something."

"Tell me," Stacey said. "I was going to go look for him. I'll tell him."

"No. It's fine."

Gurbaksh laughed. "What did you just call him?" he asked Ottilie.

"Baruch."

"Hah! No one calls him that. He tells everyone that his name is Barry." Gurbaksh put two of the drinks down on my dad's car, the condensation rolling off of them and pooling near one of the vents in the hood. I knew what was coming next. "But everyone at school calls him Yo-Yo Fag."

Ottilie barked out a mean laugh.

"You poor kid," Stacey said. There was nothing worse than the sympathy of my dad's waitress.

"It's cool," I shrugged.

"It's super messed up is what it is. There was even a teacher who called him that." Gurbaksh sipped at his drink, made a grimace, and swapped it out for one of the others. "Like it's crazy."

And then Ottilie said the thing I was hoping to never hear from her ever. "Yo-Yo fag, huh?"

I took the drink Gurbaksh rejected and drank it down as fast as I could. I wanted it to be a growth serum, something that would affect me on a cellular level and make me grow a thousand feet tall, destroying the barn, smashing the drinks, and allowing me to stomp away ten thousand yards at a stride.

"Jesus, you okay?" Gurbaksh was pounding me on my back.

"What the hell was that?"

"I think that one was Southern Comfort and 7-Up."

"That was awful."

Stacey laughed. "I used to drink in barns like this all the time growing up." She stretched her arms out above her head. "You all don't know how lucky you are. These were like the best times of my life doing this."

I snatched a wine cooler from her. It was fruity with a little alcohol burn. Like a Popsicle that had gone bad.

Ottilie opened the door on my dad's car and started the motor.

"Are we driving somewhere?" Gurbaksh laughed.

"We're listening to some radio," she said.

She turned on the rock station from Columbus. A Tears for Fears song was on.

"You know your friend won't let me touch his turban," Stacey announced. "Like how can you go around wearing a turban and not let people touch it? It's rude." She ended her little statement with a curt nod, like she'd limned out some important and eternal rule of the world. "I love this band," Stacey said next, her posture collapsing from moral arbiter to wiggling puppy.

"Me too. Have you seen the video?" Ottilie and Stacey leaned together and compared notes on who was hottest in the band.

Gurbaksh leaned up next to me and rubbed my neck. "You getting anywhere with her?"

"A gentleman doesn't kiss and tell."

"And since you're not a gentleman, I'm going to guess you haven't even made the first move."

"I just don't know how to talk to her. My brain stops working and my mouth is all stupid. I asked her what her favorite subject in school was."

"Jesus. You're worse off than I thought." He sipped from his drink, almost successfully hiding his grimace at the taste. "Have you considered that she's out of your league? Like maybe for your first time dating, a black girl is a little too much for you."

"Who said this is my first time dating?"

Gurbaksh laughed. "Whatever slow dance you might have had at sleepaway camp doesn't count here. This is a damn almost-woman."

Stacey and Ottilie shrieked, jumped up and down and started dancing.

"I'm just saying talking to girls is difficult enough for you. Talking to a black person might not need to be added to that difficulty."

"She's half black."

"Then you're thinking you'll just talk to the white half?"

We leaned against the idling car and watched the girls dancing.

"Man, this wine cooler is strong," I said. My head was woozy. If this was drunk, it sure took no time to get there.

The girls had fallen on top of each other laughing. How old was Stacey? There seemed an indeterminate age between seniors in high school and my mom's age that I couldn't place women in. What was a woman of twenty, or twenty-eight, or thirty-five to a fourteen-year-old? All the same wash of distance and impossibility. Complications and maturities and issues I wouldn't be able to pick out of a lineup. The women in the Sears catalog—standing around in their underwear with descriptions and prices next to them—seemed of another race of human. Placid icy stares I tried not to meet as I jerked off to their smooth hairless bodies. The panty section was a series of disembodied crotches all in the same pose with different panties offering varying levels of coverage. Women's crotches lined up like they were guitars at a music store. Jerking off to them made me feel awful.

"How often do you beat it?" Gurbaksh asked.

Dammit. Had I been speaking out loud?

On the ground, Ottilie was laughing hysterically and shaking her head at something Stacey had asked. Stacey turned to us and shouted, "Either of y'all ever huffed gas?"

"Jesus," Gurbaksh said. And I saw every nightmare he'd had about moving to Central Ohio play out in his posture. This was a long way from Toronto. Here were the white people he was afraid of, the gangly-limbed bad-teethed tobacco-chewing gas-huffers.

Stacey hunted around the barn until she came up with an oily rag and the gas can. "We used to do this all the time at parties when I was a kid."

She cleared the drinks off of the car, the glass tinkling as it broke on the concrete. She moved sloppily. We were all so damn drunk. It was crazy. Stacey unscrewed and tossed the nozzle and wrapped the rag around the opening. "Dare me," she said. Her eyes were wild. "I can't do it unless you dare me."

I hadn't noticed before how small her teeth were. Little worn-down yellowish nubs in an expanse of gum. How many generations of oral health neglect were there in her smile? Was she related to the forever failing Randy Colton or the couples at the County Fair who put their hands in the back pockets of each other's jean shorts or the guy who'd beat his dog in front of the school bus? Was there a world of poor whites huffing gas and beating their animals going on concurrently with my own? Like a Narnia setup and we'd just fallen through the back end of the cupboard? Tiny the janitor guarded the door and underneath him, pale as worms, the descendants of the people whose ambitions went only as far as Ohio, a people who named most everything in the language of the Algonquin people they exterminated.

"I dare the hell out of you," Gurbaksh said. He was steely. It was like his drink had turned his personality rigid. He was staring at Stacey with contempt.

She hunched over the gas can, her legs splayed out, and she wet her lips and bent down to the red dented can and there was a loud grinding sound and my dad's voice, shouting, and other men shouting and the garage door opening.

"Are you kids trying to die in here?" my dad said, coughing and waving his arms. "You can't have a car running in a closed garage. This is how people commit suicide." He reached into his car and snapped the ignition off.

We stumbled out onto the yard laughing. The fresh air came into me in big coughing gulps. I collapsed dizzy onto the lawn and Gurbaksh and Ottilie did the same on either side of me. She was laughing. The fact that we could have accidentally died seemed unbearably funny to all of us.

Dad grabbed Stacey and shook her. "I've been looking everywhere for you."

Stacey said something to my dad which I couldn't hear. My dad replied, "There are rules for a reason." And he dragged her away. My eyes were liquid and dreamy but I saw her reach up and run her fingers through his hair. I saw him push her hand away. I saw her kiss his temple.

"What the hell happened to your arm?"

Gurbaksh had his thumb close enough to the burn on my bicep to make it hurt all over again.

"Somebody's cigarette," I said.

"Damn," he said. "People are just careless with their portable fire sticks."

"I'm also short and wearing a shirt with no sleeves." The cool night air wrapped around us. Ottilie's laughter had ebbed to intermittent giggles. The looming issue of contacting her father and getting her home was too much for my brain to handle. I wanted to just lie there and enjoy the alcohol and asphyxia-induced high sitting next to my friend and Ottilie.

"Fire meets skin," Gurbaksh said. "Doesn't seem like a fair fight."

My mother's laughter burbled inside the house. I was sure she was laughing at me.

CHAPTER 30

As I MADE MY WAY TO BED, I wandered through the party-crumpled rooms. I picked bits of meat or cookies off of napkins and stuffed them in my mouth, I sipped drinks I found left behind on tables, on bookshelves, on the ground. I kept seeing Stacey kissing my dad's temple, seeing my dad shake her. My head and my stomach both felt awful.

The party staff were folding tables, the DJ was putting records back into their sleeves. In the den, Trevor was wiping off his silver bartender tools, wrapping them carefully in cloth napkins, and stacking them in an old milk crate.

"Hey, buddy," he hissed at me.

"What do you need?"

"You're the kid of the house, right? I need to talk to your dad." He wasn't that much taller than me. Just a cummerbund and a mullet of a man, really.

"He's taking some girl home."

"You kidding? I need to get paid."

I shrugged my shoulders. "I'm going to bed."

"Where's your mom?"

"I don't know."

"Somebody's gotta pay me," he mumbled to his little vials of bitters.

I went upstairs. Before I went to bed I knocked softly on my parents' door. There was no response. I pushed it open and saw two

121

silhouettes wrestling in the bed. A blanket was flushed out and soared over the two figures. I giggled. My dad wasn't sleeping with Stacey. He was here with Mom.

I heard my mother scream, "No, Baruch. Oh, sweet boy.'"

And then I heard Mr. Singh say, "Don't you lock doors here?"

CHAPTER 31

THE NEXT DAY MY MOTHER went on one of her trips. This time though she was across town, staying with the Singhs.

My dad didn't talk about it. The night of the party I heard him come home late. I laid in my bed pretending I was asleep. He cracked open the door and stood there. I could feel the triangle of light coming from the hallway. I moaned and turned over, making it as natural as possible. And then the door closed. Something happened at that moment. Something that could have passed between us, some small intimacy that was possible only at that millisecond. And I realized it immediately after he shut the door. I wanted to jump up as soon as it was closed and try to recover whatever I could, but the shame of faking sleep stopped me. A rut of behavior was wedged between us in that microscopic instant.

SECOND PART

"She . . . left me the way people leave a hotel room."
—Toni Morrison, *The Bluest Eye*

CHAPTER 1

ON MONDAY, we watched the 1974 version of Gatsby. Robert Redford and Mia Farrow. All pastels and soft focus. The fact that the biggest best-looking actors get cast as Daisy and Gatsby is an example of everyone misreading the book. But Francis Ford Coppola wrote the screenplay, which is interesting, because, if you think about it, *The Godfather II*, which Coppola wrote and directed and which also came out in 1974, is all about the Italian immigrant experience around the time that Gatsby takes place, someone new to New York who becomes very wealthy in a criminal enterprise. Are they the same movie? Not the Al Pacino/Cuba brother-killing stuff but the Robert De Niro rise-to-infamy stuff. Is Gatsby an immigrant story? Some guy who comes to the country and sees it for what it is: a brutal form of capitalism that chews up and kills anyone not at the top. American capitalism is especially brutal in that it was built by slaves, financed by banks who financed slave owners, and its founding documents were written by slave owners who said everyone is equal. An immigrant would be the only person who would see this hypocrisy for what it is and realize that the laws only applied to poor people.

So stop being poor as soon as possible.

Also, I don't know why I'm just noticing this for the first time, but Daisy and Tom have a kid. A little kid but a kid nonetheless. Shouldn't people with kids maybe not act like fucking self-involved idiots? No wonder Daisy wants her daughter to be a fool. The only way to be an American is to be a fool. The only way to be a kid is to be a fool.

"Hey, Yo-Yo Fag," Mitch Macdougal hisses at me. "Why're you sweating so badly?"

"Sorry," I said. And I don't know why I said it or what I was apologizing for.

CHAPTER 2

I came home to a note Mom had left me in the mailbox. She apologized. She said that sometimes parents had to take a break. She said that she didn't want me to ever think that she didn't love me or that any of this was my fault.

Why would I think it was my fault?

Now I couldn't help but think about how maybe this was all my fault.

There was a knock on the door. Trevor the bartender stood there. Without his little sign and his half-tux, he was sad and gray-complexioned, like he was sick or something.

"Is your dad home?" he asked.

"No."

"When do you expect him?"

"Shouldn't Mr. Singh have paid you?"

"I don't care who pays me. I just haven't been paid." He wiped at his upper lip where a small amount of spittle had collected.

"I'm pretty sure it's not my dad's fault you haven't been paid."

"Listen, kid," he said, and tried to push his way into the house. I quickly locked the screen door. And that small amount of machismo had exhausted him and he fell back as if I had kicked him in the nuts. "I don't want any trouble here. Just tell your dad I came by." He reached into his wallet and pulled out one of his business cards and tried to wedge it into the door but it kept falling down until it was a folded-up mess. He ended up putting it under the mat. "This is pretty important. I'm an independent vendor."

"Sure. Okay." I closed the front door and locked it. Then I went through the house and locked all of the other doors before hiding in the front room. He didn't leave. He stood there kind of deflated and then sat down on the porch swing.

He was there for an hour.

CHAPTER 3

I STARTED RUNNING around the block containing the grocery store across the street every night. It was quiet, almost no cars at all. Just the cold fluorescent tents of the parking lot. The air was cool and the leaves ticked and the cicadas argued endlessly as men unloaded semitrucks into the grocery store's massive rear doors. The men sat on the loading dock and smoked. I'd run by and five minutes later I'd run by again.

One night one of the grocery men waved me over. He was tall and heavy. His skin was nicked in a million different ways and his nose was a dollop of mangled flesh. He wiped his hands on his pants and grabbed me by the shoulders. He said, "Stop bouncing. Keep it low. You're wasting too goddamn much energy going up. That energy should be pushing you forward." He took his hands away from me and motioned for me to get back to it. The smell of mustard from his sandwich clung to him. "And get some real shoes for chrissake."

This was the most significant human interaction I had for about two weeks.

CHAPTER 4

ALSO . . .

I never called Ottilie after the party. I figured her dad would be mad. I figured I couldn't really be of much interest to her. There are kits, like model airplanes and cars, and their included instructions are frequently inscrutable, but you always have the picture on the box to go on. You know what you're building because you see the image on the box.

My parents' marriage was over. I was a mess of parts on an unlabeled box. I didn't know who I was or who I was supposed to be. I figured I was doing her a favor by staying away. I would only make a mess of their lives.

Dad parked himself in the living room each day after work and watched TV. He wouldn't eat unless I made him something. We ate a lot of spaghetti while watching whatever was on TV. He was silent. It was like living with a remote control, a lump of inert plastic that'd change channels whenever it wanted.

CHAPTER 5

RHEUMY-EYED MR. MORRIS handed out a mimeographed sheet of the topics for the essays we had to write, due before Thanksgiving break. He had lost about thirty pounds since the beginning of the school year and one of those purple spots on his scalp had gotten huge and now looked like a birthmark the size of a Tic Tac container on his cheek. He told us it was the flu.

Each essay must include quotes from two secondary sources. Essays must be formatted and proofread and free of grammatical and usage errors to receive full credit.

1. Write a 750-word essay on the topic of tragic love and how it applies to Daisy and Gatsby. Feel free to use other examples from literature (Romeo & Juliet, Ethan Frome, etc.). You will receive a failing grade if you mention Madonna and Sean Penn or George Michael and Brooke Shields.

2. Write a 750-word essay on the meaning of the green light that Gatsby stares at and how it relates to Gatsby's own desire for wealth. Think about capitalism on this one.

3. Write a 750-word essay on the meaning of the billboard of Dr. T. J. Eckleburg and its enormous eyes and its relationship to Christianity during the Jazz Age. Is Fitzgerald maybe positing that God is as dead to the Jazz Age as those eyes on that billboard?

Mr. Morris deserved all the shitty essays he'd have to read.

CHAPTER 6

IN MY SCIENCE CLASS, we all had new workbooks about the history of the shuttle program. Mr. Reynolds was wearing his NASA hat and pin and was patrolling the aisles as we completed the activities.

We calculated the thrust necessary to pull free of the Earth's gravity and figured out how much we would weigh on the moon. There was a maze where we had to get a spaceman out on a spacewalk back to his ship.

It wasn't a walk at all of course. It was more like a swim in a substance that no one knew how to swim in. Your limbs totally awkward because of your space suit. Any little tear capable of destroying you. Any little push enough to send you somersaulting forever into space. The spaceman had a big smile on his face as he hung there in zero g. His giant space-suit arm held up in a wave.

Thanksgiving was two weeks away and Christmas loomed large. I had no idea what it would look like. Who would attend? Where? And why?

I had no idea how much shopping I needed to get done. Or if I needed to be writing a wish list. No one had asked me for one. My dad left me checks whenever I asked him for anything. I had new running shoes, a Walkman, and was totally outfitted in cold-weather gear, so I could keep running every night.

If you became separated from your spaceship and were spinning and you knew you were going to die as soon as your air ran out, would it be possible to enjoy the view? Because you'd know you were the only human being to ever get to see all the things you were seeing. I wonder if you could calm down enough, give up the hope that you'd be rescued, give up the hope that you could do anything to change the outcome, and instead accept what was happening, know that you only had this many breaths, know that you could control nothing, and marvel at how incredible it was to be alive in space, hurtling not towards but through oblivion. If the worst had already happened, wouldn't some great weight be lifted? Like you didn't have to worry anymore, instead you could wonder at how your toes felt as they lost their warmth, at the very particular feeling of your lungs freezing.

Mr. Reynolds wanted us to hurry so he could tell us again about almost becoming the first teacher sent up into space.

The spaceman in my workbook hung there in space, waving at me, smiling.

CHAPTER 7

I THINK I MIGHT HAVE GIVEN the impression that the results of that party, indeed my brief friendship with Gary Singh and failed court-ship of Ottilie Regan, had been all that had occupied me during the entirety of the fall.

I read a lot of comic books. I read a bunch of back issues of *X-Men*, nearly the entirety of the Dark Phoenix saga, where Jean Grey, Marvel Girl, gets cosmic powers and then becomes omnipotent and then evil and then dead, killed by her own teammates. But then she comes back to life, y'know, 'cause her name is Phoenix. And then in more recent issues Rachel Summers, Jean Grey's daughter from an alternate future, shows up and raises all sorts of hell because she hadn't known her mother in her timeline and here is her mother, walking around, oblivious to a daughter she never had. It was so fucked up. The daughter wanting connection and the mother unaware she was a mother.

Maybe in another timeline, Mom and I had a different rela-tionship.

Dad and I went to see an encore screening of *Back to the Future* because we'd missed it during the summer. Dad spent the whole drive home railing against how love and capitalistic success were linked. Fix your parents' marriage, get a new truck. He said that any movie in which the teleology of love is that people were made for each other was suspect, that marriage is much more than the courting but Hollywood can't show you the other parts of marriage because it's boring, hard work. Dad ranted all the way into the house about vows and fidelity and movies about marriage making it to be all about uxoriousness. And I think he was still going when I closed my door and went to bed. It was hard to see a person use their whole vocabulary to distract themselves from their pain.

In one day in November, I drank two suitcases of Dr Pepper.

I developed and nurtured a crush on Jennifer (never Jenny) McComber, who sat beside me in study hall, and who smelled like Hubba Bubba. But then I heard she gave Randy Price a BJ on a field trip to the science museum.

After detention one day, I wandered the empty halls of the school and dared myself to go into the girl's bathroom. There was a vending machine for pads on one of the walls. I slid a nickel into it and took the little package home with me and hid it under my pillow. I felt perverted and it crept across my skull in spidery shivers and I blushed so hard that it hurt.

The school passed a rule against torn jeans.

Randy Colton and Tommy Williams came up with a game they could play after gym class, when we were supposed to be changing back into our regular clothes in the locker room. They'd wait until the majority of us were bent over, wrestling our jeans on, and Tommy Williams would jump on Randy's back with his legs stuck out either side of him and Randy would spin down the narrow aisles scattering everyone. One time when he was trying to escape them, Bryce Palatini ended up tripping and splitting his head open on the concrete floor. There was blood everywhere. The locker room smelled like bleach for a week.

The drama club did a performance of *Free to Be You and Me* that we all were required to attend. Raelynn Thompson got sick in the middle of it and vomited on the stage.

Porky Boxwell ran a little black-market business of Now and Laters that I accidentally tattled on, making a mortal enemy of Porky Boxwell. That meant Randy Colton, the giant, was now my enemy as well. But he was so big that it was easy to avoid him in the halls.

I bought Run-D.M.C.'s *King of Rock* album, which was popular, which would've made my mom happy, if she wasn't off living with Mr. Singh. It was good music to run to, though I had to keep my head very still so the headphones wouldn't slide off.

CHAPTER 8

My paper on Gatsby:

What Eyes Can't See Even
When They're Looking Right At It:
The Role of Looking in *The Great Gatsby*

Eyes are an important part of *The Great Gatsby*. The way people see (and are seen) is an essential storytelling strategy that Fitzgerald employs. Fitzgerald lets us know that this is an important part of his book by including a billboard of lifeless eyes for an expired optometrist's practice. This would seem like a clumsy attempt to create a symbol and some people have tried to make an absurd argument about the eyes of God and the theological moral deadness inside the book. But Fitzgerald is up to something way more interesting than a simple moral argument.

There are two very important moments of Gatsby looking. One is his looking across the bay at the green light at the end of the Buchanan's dock. This is an important moment because he is being observed by Nick Carraway without his knowledge. Gatsby just wants any kind of intimacy with Daisy and if he has to settle on a light stuck on the end of a pier, well that's a whole lot closer than he's been since he last saw her in Louisville, Kentucky. The color of the light doesn't matter here.

It's the ardency of his gaze. He's been staring at Daisy since he first saw her, during the war, at Oxford, all while amassing his fortune. One could say he's been staring at Daisy for so long from so far away that he doesn't ever really see her in the present day. Right?

The second time and even more important moment of Gatsby staring at Daisy is after the accident that kills Myrtle Wilson. Gatsby is waiting in the bushes for Daisy to come out and he's staring at her house. He's out there waiting for her to honor a promise that she won't ever honor. The thing Gatsby doesn't see is that Daisy is married and is a mother. He can't even imagine the conversations being had in the Buchanan house. He doesn't see her as anything but that girl from Louisville and this is his mistake. Gatsby has lived his life trying to assemble a future that would impress a woman from his past and he assumes she's the same person from those days, stuck in amber waiting for him to be worthy of her.

He can't see across the bay, he can't see through the walls of her house. His eyes are as dull and blind as the billboard of Dr. T. J. Eckleburg. And this is the biggest thing that Fitzgerald is saying, I think, that we can stare as much as we want to but we can't stare our way into someone else's marriage or into someone else's life. Our eyes are the wrong organ to be using. Gatsby should be listening rather than staring. Daisy is a mom (a crappy one but a mom nonetheless). And since Gatsby doesn't ask any questions about Daisy's life he loses her because of this simple fact. The years have changed Daisy. Gatsby has used those years to make him someone who could impress the young woman in his past. As a result, he sees nothing and is left trying to stare across distances and through walls to make her someone she isn't. And even though Tom is a horrible husband (like literally the worst husband ever), they've spent too many years together to just give up entirely. At least Tom sees her or has seen her through the years, there's an intimacy to Tom's looking, while Gatsby's looking is too remote (across the years, across the bay), too distant to matter.

In conclusion, the billboard of Dr. T. J. Eckleburg is less than a common literary symbol but rather a signpost to Fitzgerald's narrative strategy. And it's through this signpost that we see the bigger issue that Fitzgerald is up to, that of the limits of covetousness. You can spend your life trying to impress other people but Gatsby could have been better served to realize that he didn't ever really see Daisy, even when she was right next to him. I think the whole book would be better if it was narrated by Tom and Daisy's kid.

Because that kid is probably really and truly fucked.

(I think this is 750 words. But if it's not, oh well. My title should count as part of the 750 words. I'm just saying. How many kids know how to do a colonated title? Also I didn't use any sources because I wanted to write something original. Also I hope you get better.)

CHAPTER 9

ON THE MONDAY BEFORE THANKSGIVING BREAK, I was called out of English class to come to the office. We had been watching a version of *A Christmas Carol* partly because it was originally written by Charles Dickens and partly because none of us gave a shit about school because it was so close to break. I looked at Mr. Morris to see if this was going to be about my essay. But he was too busy trying to find a dry spot on his handkerchief to blow his nose into to even notice.

In the office sat Mr. Singh. He was wearing a navy turban, a pink shirt, and a scarf so loudly printed that my eyes were deafened.

"I thought we could take a drive to Columbus," he said, with the vice-principal standing there, his head bobbing like a buoy in placid water. "We can buy your mother a present."

It was a little too easy for someone not my parent to take me out of school. The scandal of my family had become common enough knowledge to make the administration numbly compliant with any fresh new outrage.

Ohioans are like that. So polite in the presence of obvious sin, so nasty when it's just rumored.

I got my coat and my backpack from my locker. It hadn't been vandalized in months—a shiny place from where it'd been scrubbed so many times. Maybe that was the final vandalism. Something done so often that the marks of cleaning had permanently scarred it. I missed the vandalism. It was such easy drama.

I met Mr. Singh in the parking lot. His red Saab had been freshly washed, just light marks of slush and salt on the wheel wells. Against the snow-covered football field, the car looked like a zit on an albino.

As soon as I got in the car, Mr. Singh stood on the gas pedal. The car took off so fast I was pushed back into the seat. We both sat there quietly as he danced through the half dozen or so intersections between school and the highway. It wasn't until we got onto 23 South and he levered the car into fifth gear that he began to speak—almost as if he couldn't speak unless he was free of shifting gears.

"I thought we should get some lunch and speak man to man," he said.

"I didn't think we were really going shopping."

"Your mother is quite heartbroken that you won't speak to her."

"Do you have to drive so fast?" I said. "It's icy out."

"I used to drive in Canada." He waved his hands dismissively at the world outside the windshield. "This is simple."

He gunned the engine to make his point.

"I need you to know something about me. I think it will be helpful as we all come to terms with this new situation. I am not the sort of man who comes and snatches women from their husbands. I am not that man. I love your mother and she loves me." He downshifted right before we hit a hill and the car flew for a moment before wiggling down on its suspension. "And she has for a long time."

He then told me the most amazing story.

He had been an engineer with the Indian Air Force, modifying and maintaining the Folland Gnats for combat. "Terrible hydraulics on those things, absolutely the pits. I have scars on my hands from staying up late fixing the damn things." He had been a part of the war of 1971 against Pakistan.

"It took thirteen short days. The shortest war ever. Took out the Butcher of Bengal, a very very bad man."

He told me about the great pilot Nirmal Jit Singh Sekhon, who held his own against six of the Pakistani Canadair Sabres, scoring hits on two of them before being shot down.

"The Sabres started strafing the base and he got in his Gnat, took off, and he engaged them. Took off during an attack. The man was fearless. The whole battle was done at treetop level. Do you understand? Skimming the trees. Outmaneuvering six other planes. Defended the Srinagar air base, by himself."

There was the Battle of Boyra with PT-76 tanks invading East Pakistan and the Gnats providing air support.

"We called them the Sabre Slayers."

Mr. Singh had emerged with medals and was promised a prestigious posting. There were politics at work though that he'd been unaware of.

"Probably did not shake the right hands at parties, did not flirt enough or flirted too much with a boss's wife. Badmaash and dacoits, the lot of them."

He never got to assume the post. And then an old subordinate turned on him and spread vicious rumors about him, saying he was incompetent and an idler. The rumors had curdled the opportunities even with the private aeronautical companies. When Indira Gandhi's government announced their Emergency, he decided he had to flee the country.

"Gurbaksh was coming home from school spouting such nationalist nonsense. I could not envision a future for him in a country run by that woman. My wife refused to even consider leaving. She didn't believe Nehru's daughter could do such evil."

The rush of the world suddenly stopped. Mr. Singh was out of the car and putting his coat on before I realized we'd parked.

"I'm sorry I never asked. Do you like Chi-Chi's? It's Mexican."

Inside the restaurant, Mr. Singh ordered the chicken fajitas. For two. Without consulting me. The waiter snapped the menus from us before I realized what happened.

"We arrived in Toronto where I had some family members who hadn't turned their backs on me for abandoning my wife." He folded his hands in front of him reverentially. "It is the greatest regret of my life leaving her."

In Toronto, he couldn't get an engineering job because he couldn't produce his transcripts so the first job he got was as a caddy at a golf course.

"I knew nothing of the game. A friend of a friend made the connection for me. I worked strictly for tips. For the first week, I thought the names on the players' balls were their own. I was saying, 'Good shot, Mr. Titleist.' 'Excellent work, Mr. Slazenger.' And one day I was working for a young woman who I thought was named Mrs. Callaway."

When he said this, I remembered the notes that came with the flowers and the food the night of my dad's party. The ones my mom clutched in the shower.

"That was my mom."

He looked surprised. "You are quick, little Baruch. Yes, it was your mother. I was taken with her immediately. I used every excuse I could find to draw her into conversation. She was a terrible golfer and I was a miserable caddy so we had plenty of time to talk.

"I had never fallen in love before, you need to realize. My wife and I were a match that made sense and while we were fond of each other and were good partners, I'd never known this . . . hunger for another person's company."

Our drinks came—mine a Dr Pepper, his a hot tea into which he dumped five packets of sugar and half of his creamer tureen. Mr. Singh reset himself. Maybe realizing talking about his hunger for my mom might have been a skosh inappropriate.

"We had dinner that night. As well as the next night. She'd have business dinners each night but she would not eat at these affairs in order to eat with me. She left before I ever learned her real name. I always called her Mrs. Callaway, to which she always laughed and never corrected me.

"I knew she worked for Marriott. So Gurbaksh and I emigrated to America and traveled to Marriott cities, spending time in each searching for a woman whose name I didn't know. In America I was able to get engineering jobs and I built on each job each time we moved to a new city."

The wild sizzling of our fajitas came through the restaurant, quieting all the enchilada- and quesadilla-eaters into paroxysms of envy. The mad presentation and spectacle of the Chi-Chi's fajita cast iron with Sterno underneath was one of the most hedonistic things I'd ever seen. It made everyone in the restaurant want to be you. It was weird to think of my mom in love. I'd thought Dad and her—actually I'm not sure I ever thought of them being in love. They argued a lot and Mom was gone a lot. How much does anyone want to know about their parents' marriage? It was like the weather. It affected your whole day but you've got no control over it.

"Careful," our server said. "It's hot."

We loaded up our flour tortillas with meat, peppers, and onions, heaping on shredded cheese and tomatoes. We were three bites into our second helping before I got up the nerve to ask him the question I'd been meaning to ask him the entire drive but somehow never found the perfect place to ask.

"So how is my mom doing?"

CHAPTER 10

MR. SINGH DROPPED me back at school in time for eighth period. I had the fajita leftovers in one plastic bag and the birthday gift Mr. Singh had helped me buy for Mom (I'd suggested a nightgown, he showed me these lacy numbers that he thought she might like, I got her a stuffed Garfield). It probably wasn't the best gift but Mr. Singh was rushing me, saying that we needed to be getting back and my thoughts went all muddy. My mom had no use for a stuffed Garfield but then I never really had any use for South Korean haute couture punk rock T-shirts.

Also she wasn't much of a mother. Not to me at least.

The bell had rung and the halls were filled with people. I went straight to study hall with my bags of presents and fajitas and homework. It was like being famous. I felt like one of those fancy ladies in movies during a shopping spree, awkwardly laden with bags. I slid down the aisle to my seat. I waited for someone to whisper at me the question of where I'd been.

"Lunch and a little shopping in Columbus," I was ready to say.

Jennifer McComber sat next to me. She had a nose that could slice deli meat and an overbite that could open a pop bottle but she was still really attractive. I don't know how people like her do it. Be a beautiful ugly person. Most good-looking people were ugly beautiful. Somehow she was able to do some corporeal alchemy and in her jean jacket and gummy bracelets she was radiant most days in braces and sprayed-stiff bangs.

"Hey, Yo-Yo Fag," she whispered to me, like I had willed it to happen.

"What?" I asked.

"Keep it down, morons." The guy up front was the baseball coach and this was his job: study hall monitor. Everyone called him Coach Study Hall, even to his face. There were at least three girls he was rumored to be fucking, which was totally unfair. How could any of us compete with a year playing AA-ball and a Datsun 300ZX? Anyway, he was notorious for sending kids to Saturday school on the most minor infractions so neither Jennifer McComber or I talked for fifteen minutes to let the storm pass. I used the time to practice my line. "Oh, just lunch and a little shopping in Columbus." "I jetted to Columbus and back, y'know, lunch and some shopping. Did I miss anything?" "I dashed out to Columbus for some Mexican food. Did a little shopping too while I was there."

"Hey," she hissed at me. "You're leaking."

She pointed at my Chi-Chi's bag. The corner was dark brown with liquid. I jumped up to throw it out.

"Do you need to ask for permission for something?" Coach Study Hall shouted.

Out of my seat with the leaky bag clutched to my chest, I froze. While I searched for the words I needed, laughter started rolling through the room. I felt warmth spreading across my belly and down my pants as the fajita liquid drizzled down my body.

"Jesus, man. Have some self-respect," Coach Study Hall said.

The wet spot on my clothes was continental in proportion. "It's fajita juice," I said to the laughing room. "It's fajita juice. It's from my lunch."

"Go to the bathroom and clean yourself up," Coach Study Hall said, throwing the hall pass at my chest so hard I got pushed back. I tripped on my backpack and fell on my ass. The laughter got louder.

I stood up and ran from the room. But in the hallway, teachers and students who had heard the laughter and poked their heads out of their rooms started laughing when they saw me. I ran to the bathroom and stayed there until the final bell rang. When I figured the halls would be empty, I left and went to pick my stuff up. On my desk was a note from the coach telling me to show up at 9:00 a.m. for Saturday school after break, on account of not returning the hall pass in a timely manner. I grabbed my backpack and fled the scene.

I don't know when I realized that I left the bag with my mom's present in it.

CHAPTER 11

I TOOK THE SHORTCUT along the train tracks. People said there were Satanists that partied up there on the trestle but I kind of couldn't believe that they'd be partying at 4:00 p.m. on a Monday. Also with the grease stain on my pants walking home along the main road was not going to happen. I saw an abandoned bicycle lying beside the tracks and had enough time to formulate an ethics model that allowed me to steal it before I saw that there were two people lying together in the weeds and then it took me a little too long to realize that they were having sex. And too long after that to realize that it was Holly Trowbridge and Randy Colton and way too long before I realized I should stop staring. I walked by as ninja-silent as I could. But I was either going to go on the ties or on the chunky gravel. The ties were quiet but too close. The chunky gravel was farther away but too noisy. And there was no way I was getting out of this.

I walked on the farthest side of the ties away from them. I tried not to look but I also needed to monitor them. If they chased me I was going to need every last sliver of a head start. Randy's big white bottom was flexing and releasing and Holly had one of her hands grabbed onto his ass, with one of her fingers jammed up his butthole. I only half saw this. But Randy kept on saying, "Up my ass. Up my ass. So good up my ass." I let his words fill me in on what she was doing back there. I didn't believe that you could talk a girl into doing something like that. Or that you'd want a girl to do something like that. I only knew my own butthole from wiping, washing, and a distant memory of thermometers. Also wasn't Holly Trowbridge Porky Boxwell's girlfriend and wasn't Randy Porky's cousin? I shut my eyes hard and tried not to breathe.

Just as I was about halfway past them, how could I not look? I mean, sex was a complete mystery to me and I had Cinemax. It was the animating subtext of my life and there it was by the side of the train tracks, fifteen feet away from me. Also there were two of the scariest people I knew and they were totally vulnerable. Totally wrapped up in some cocoon of their own making. Oblivious to the snow, the cold, the exposure.

I tripped on a tie. I just staggered a little but I was so convinced they'd heard me that I said, "Sorry." And then I ran. I never looked back so I don't know how long they chased me for.

CHAPTER 12

THE NEXT DAY ON THE BUS, Holly didn't look at me, even though I tried to give her a little wave that meant, "I am so not going to say anything about you tickling your boyfriend's cousin's asshole near the train tracks yesterday." I wanted her to know that I wouldn't rat them out.

When Porky got on three stops later, she said, "There's my lover-boy," and kissed him so hard and for so long that the bus driver yelled at them three times to get them to stop.

"There's no PDA on the bus, children. Keep it in your pants," she said to the long rearview mirror above her.

I turned in a slip about the Garfield doll to the main office to be read over the PA during morning announcements but my mind couldn't really focus past the fact that I was going to get my ass beaten by Randy Colton. It was going to happen in gym. It was going to happen in the locker room. If I skipped gym, he'd beat me up after school. If I skipped school, he'd just wait until I came back. If I switched schools, he'd weaponize his vast inbred family to come after me. Everyone that is except Porky. Porky might beat my ass just because I was the witness to his betrayal. And maybe Randy would help Porky kick my ass because they'd heard that line about blood being thicker than water and they wanted to test the viscosity of my blood.

We got to school and my head was oscillating so much that my neck started to hurt. I would have no chance against Randy so I don't know why it was so important for me to be on the lookout. Maybe I just wanted to see it coming.

"Barry," someone behind me yelled. I bunched my shoulders so hard that I heard a pop. "Barry," the person said again. I opened my eyes. Gurbaksh stood in front of me; his face in that expression that's tired of me being so weird.

"Did my dad take you to lunch yesterday?" he asked.

I nodded while peeking around him.

"In Columbus?"

I nodded again.

"Next time, say no," he said, while punching my shoulder with his index finger. "He tell you about being a war hero? You know he lies, right? Why can't anyone see this? You and your mom are such suckers."

"I'm sorry," I heard a voice a lot like mine saying. It didn't continue so I don't know if I was apologizing for going to Chi-Chi's or excusing myself from the conversation or saying that he had the wrong person—*I'm sorry, you must have me confused with someone else.* I really don't know what I meant by it. And I didn't have any time to find out because a giant hand dropped on my shoulder.

"This guy bothering you, Little Psycho?"

I turned around and there hovering over us with his close-set eyes burning holes into Gurbaksh was Randy Colton.

"Go away, raghead. Don't bother my friends."

Gurbaksh wiped his mouth and repeated, "Next time, say no."

Randy Colton punched Gurbaksh in the stomach.

"The fuck he cares about what you say to anyone," Randy said. "Fucking sandnigger."

Gurbaksh slung his backpack off and jumped at Randy, simultaneously a totally badass and dumbass move. He got in a couple of swings at Randy's head before Randy picked him up and slammed him to the ground. And then did it again. And then stomped on

Gurbaksh's chest a couple of times. A crowd had formed around us. Chanting, "Fight! Fight! Fight!" basically begging for a teacher to break it up. Gurbaksh wrapped himself around Randy's legs to stop him from stomping him. Randy lost his balance and crashed, his head bouncing off the hard ground. Gurbaksh climbed up onto Randy's chest and punched him in the throat and the face. There was blood on the linoleum. Honest-to-God blood. Whose it was I had no idea.

Coach Study Hall pushed through the crowd and wrestled Gurbaksh off of Randy, putting him in a sleeper hold and shaking him a couple of times like a dog does to a kitten it's caught.

The vice-principal blew his whistle several times and yelled, "Disperse, students. Disperse." And everyone ran away.

Randy stood up shakily. The back of his head was a gory mess. He reached behind and felt it then looked at his hand. Then he fainted.

CHAPTER 13

I STARTED BREATHING AGAIN around lunch. It was then that I realized that I had not been punched, slapped, or made fun of at all up until then. In the lunch line, one of the cafeteria ladies asked me if I was Barry. She told me she was Randy Colton's aunt Flossie and she gave me an extra slice of pizza. The pizza was rectangular and was shaped to fit the tray's largest divided section, so the extra piece was placed chiastically on top of the other one. And she was so shocked to hear that I didn't know about dipping my pizza in ranch dressing that she gave me four extra packets and then waved me through the line.

Something very strange was going on. Randy was sent to the hospital. He'd cracked his head open badly when he fainted. And Gurbaksh was disappeared into the front office. I sat down at an empty table and pulled out the book that I picked up at the Quarter Price Books, the storefront of the remainder mill. The books there are shelter puppies waiting for the needle and I can't go in there but for wanting to rescue them all. It was a copy of *Invisible Cities* by Italo Calvino, which was a weirdo book of Marco Polo bullshitting about different cities he saw in his travels like if Scheherazade made an almanac, but it was slow reading and didn't weigh much so it was the perfect pleasure book for me. I see people with their Stephen King restaurant hamburger with all the fixings–sized paperbacks. Those books are dangerous. You could herniate a disc just picking one up and you flipped pages so quickly that you could accidentally start a fire. I liked this weirdo book. High school had made me feel like a remainder, some unpopular appendage which isn't doing at all what was expected of it. Now selling at a loss.

I was still in shock from the fight. I didn't know what any of the last twenty-four hours augured for me. I ate both slices of the pizza and when I stood up I noticed that I had spilled some of the tomato sauce on my pants. But as I scraped at it with my fingernail, I realized that it was blood. I'd gotten flecked with blood. I didn't jump in on the fight for either Randy or Gurbaksh. I didn't even try to break it up. I thought I could stand by and not get involved. But my pants got involved regardless. I was marked complicit.

Now I got to explain my stained pants to my dad.

CHAPTER 14

I WAS WALKING into my study hall at the end of the day before I realized that everyone in that room thought I'd wet myself the day before, a possibility that normally would have engulfed every one of my manic thoughts. But it didn't matter anymore. Fuck them if they wanna think whatever dumb little things that filter through their bullshit and emerge in their rinky-dink backwater consciousness. Fuck the bruise on my sternum where coach had thrown the hall pass. I was now involved in a deeper violence. Fuck a hall pass. I walked in and while there was whispering and glances shot my way, there was no laughing and no pointing.

At my desk there was a wrapped bundle and two notes. One note was written in impeccable cursive and it went: "Dear Barry, There was a mix-up yesterday and somehow I ended up with your shopping bag. It was not until I reached home that I realized my mistake. I unwrapped the package to see what it was. And after realizing that it wasn't mine, I realized that I had accidentally taken your bag on mistake. Here is your Garfield doll. I rewrapped it myself. Hope there's no hard feelings. Sincerely, Anonymouse"

It was obviously a girl's handwriting. Someone who took great pride in their cursive z's. Why else include three variations on the word "realize." Also they only misspelled one word and that was the signature, which seemed to say that the author decided against signing it until the end. Or maybe it was that they were trying to throw me off the scent by making an error because the person who wrote it never makes errors. Or it was written by a rodent seeking to conceal their identity.

The second note was from Coach Study Hall. And while it didn't apologize, it did excuse me from Saturday school on the basis that I had already learned my lesson. I was learning a lesson. A lesson of sex and violence. It turns out that when you see people doing something you can't unsee, they're more embarrassed than you are and the fact that you can't unsee what you saw establishes your new power. There's opportunity in being the person who's in the wrong place at the wrong time. I'd seen Randy's white ass and his blood within about fourteen hours.

I was nearly halfway through my freshman year; 1986 was being rolled out to the launchpad, and I was caught in a war between Randy Colton and the tribe of Coltons who were the thread sewn through our town and my ex-friend (and maybe soon to be stepbrother) Gurbaksh. I wanted each of them to lose.

CHAPTER 15

Some of us are powerless not because we're underdogs who're being kept down and shuttled to the margins. No. Some of the powerless are powerless because we cannot be trusted with power. It's like the universe preemptively strips us of power since all we'd ever do is cause others pain if we had any of it. Some of us are losers and not the loveable kind. Some of us have never lit a match without looking for someone nearby to burn.

Everyone at school wants to talk to me, wants the direct poop on the fight. I want them all to fuck off and die.

I find a note in my locker inviting me to a party at Randy's family's house on the next Saturday, like a post-Thanksgiving thing. I don't know how it got into my locker. But there it is.

I walk home, taking the long way around to avoid the train tracks. I'm in some kind of horrible funk. I don't know why I'm thinking this stuff about underdogs and loneliness and burning. It's like for most of my life I live in a submarine and sometimes it's like I need to pop my head out of the hatch. I watch way too much TV. The VCR is killing me with all the movies—every movie available at my fingertips. I don't know what it's doing to my head. I think this will be the last generation raised on screens. We'll hit a tipping point and people will turn away from the TV screen and actually talk to the person in the room.

Granted there is no one here for me to talk to.

Dad is off with his waitress friend. Mom might be on a trip, might just be shacked up down the road. No, I think with this generation what we are exploring is isolation. Everyone staring at TV screens together but being totally alone, learning how to deal with tedium, establishing outposts on the edges of loneliness. And the tide will swing and the pendulum will turn. The future is outdoors, naked and huddled on rock faces far from the storm. This is how we are preparing for life on the moon. Staring at TV screens like we're staring at the inside of our visors. On the moon we would have to live in our space suits all the time, helmets on and sealed.

I come home from school and I watch TV until it's dark enough outside and I run. I'm the fucking Lewis and Clark of teenage angst. I am first on so many mountain peaks. There might have been people who've lived here before me but I am an American and I occupied my land like no one had ever previously held honest claim to it; my pubescence was radical and new, my future form indeterminate. My sweat is amniotic fluid as I forced myself to be reborn every mile on my weekday five-mile loop. I am original. I am alone.

These are the thoughts of any moth in any cocoon ever. I am so fucking gizmo.

CHAPTER 16

THE HOUSE WAS IN HAYES COLONY, a strip of duplexes surrounding an emptied swimming pool and bordered by the train tracks with four or five acres of woods on the other side. I'd never been in a duplex before. A house split in half vertically, with families on either side. The Colton family rented duplexes in serial, so even though each house had two families they were all the same family. The party was being held in three of the duplexes. There was a small fire out in the walkway built of scraps of two-by-fours, even though it was a fairly temperate late November night. Men in wifebeaters, men without shirts, men in Browns jerseys, men in those half shirts that Johnny Depp wore in *A Nightmare on Elm Street* milled about. The women were in oversized jerseys and sweats or tube tops and booty shorts depending on their age and body type. There was a steady stream of traffic between the different houses. Someone had crawled out onto one of the low roofs and put a boom box there, blasting out Black Sabbath, Rush, and Heart, a kind of sonic compote of late-70s guitar licks and drum solos. Everything I saw and heard made me want to run away.

"Little Psycho!" Randy busted out of a screen door and jogged over to me. He still had a bandage on the back of his head and a black eye. "You showed up. I was convinced you'd pussy out." He plopped his hand on my head and directed me over to the fire. "Let's get you a beer and introduce you to people."

At the fire, an older man outfitted in a Camel Cash jacket was telling a joke. "There's these three guys called into the draft board, right? They're stripped down and each of the guys gets a bell tied to his dick. The first guy gets called up and the psychiatrist shows him a picture of a naked chick. The guy's bell goes *ding ding ding*. The psychiatrist writes something down in his file and says, 'Go on and sit on that bench there.' Next guy gets called up, right? Same thing. Picture of a naked chick and his peter starts going *ding ding ding*. 'Go on and sit over there on that bench.' Third guy gets called up. Psychiatrist shows him the same picture of the naked chick." The guy took a big swig of his beer. "Fucking silence. Not even a little ringing. Psychiatrist writes something down in his file and says, 'All right. Go sit next to those other guys on the bench.' And the guy's bell goes *ding ding ding ding ding*."

"That's my uncle John. Guy knows every joke ever. Uncle John. Uncle John. This here is Little Psycho."

"Hey, little man." Uncle John was a bear of a man. He switched his cigarette from his right to his left to give me a meaty handshake. "How's it hanging?"

"Pretty good, I guess," I said and immediately regretted it. How were you supposed to answer that dumb question?

"Hey, you know why when the hotel caught on fire the fags were the first ones out?"

"I don't."

"Cause they had their shit packed the night before, man." He laughed hard and told me to pull up a chair. "You hungry? I can get one of the girls to make you up a plate."

Randy put a cold beer against my neck and everyone laughed as I jumped.

"You ever shoot a beer, Little Psycho?" Randy asked.

"Sure," I lied. "Plenty."

"Let's do it then."

I started to open the beer and Randy clamped his hand down on mine. "No, man. First you've gotta make the hole in the bottom."

Randy took out a small knife and poked a hole near the bottom. Three of the other guys did the same. Randy handed me the knife and I struggled to pierce the can. "Here. Take mine."

He popped a hole in the can.

"All right, on the count of three you're going to put your mouth on the hole and open the can at the same time. Beer is just gonna slide down into you real quick. Ready?"

The countdown happened and everyone ducked down and then rose up. I fumbled for a while to get the can open but once I did the beer choked me and forced its way down my throat. I drank maybe a third of the beer with the rest of it spewing down my shirt. I emerged coughing and gasping and laughing. And so did everyone else. We threw our cans into the fire and everyone high-fived one another. It was actually pretty great.

People started to drift over to us, attracted by the clamor.

"Why they call you Psycho, little man? Cause you must be some serial-killer shit as small as you are."

Randy answered for me. "This little dude tore up this guidance counselor bitch's office on the second damn day of school."

The crowd laughed and someone shook my shoulder and roughed up my hair.

"I was there in the office when it happened . . ."

"Of course you were," someone shouted.

"Fuck you," Randy shouted back. "I was there and all of a sudden there's all this noise of glass breaking and shit. The principal, that dick of a vice-principal, and the little office ladies we all jumped up and opened the door and there's Little Psycho sitting on the floor, papers everywhere, her pictures broken on the floor, looking cool as shit." Randy laughed. "They basically had to carry him out of there. He got suspended before I could."

The crowd roared. The adulation combined with the beer was the best I'd felt in months.

"Good on you, Psycho man. I don't know why you're still wasting your time at that school, Randy. You're sixteen. You can leave, get you a real job."

"Maybe because we don't need another Colton with only a ninth-grade education, John."

The crowd hushed. A woman with a paper plate of food in her hand came into the circle. "You know I hate you encouraging the boy's devilishness, John. Just cause you're a failure doesn't mean you need to make sure my son follows your dumbass into poverty."

"I'm not a failure, you old cow," John shot back. "And I'm not in poverty neither. I've got a steady job."

"You're Honda poor. Making the same there that you made when you first got hired on. A salary that's great when you're eighteen isn't a great salary when you're forty-three. But you can't do anything else, so that's as good as it's gonna get for you."

"I take care of my responsibilities. I've got a boat. I travel. What the hell else do you want out of life?"

"Travel? Going to Indianapolis for the race isn't travel. You're barely leaving the state. You've got no vision." She was stabbing her cigarette at him as she spoke, its cherry sparking and tracing through the night. "You tell your stupid jokes and get wasted every weekend. Forgive me for wanting more from my boy."

She flicked her cigarette into the fire and stormed off. The crowd around the fire went dead silent. If it weren't for the AC/DC song blaring about Big Balls, you'd think we were praying.

Randy's mom slammed the screen door shut and it released us

from something. People went *ooooooooo* like the sound studio audience's make when characters kiss.

I loved her like someone would love the idea of a new opposable limb. A mother's love like that seemed impossible. All fury and devotion.

John slapped me on the shoulder, "Don't mind her. Randy's mom runs hot nowadays. Women's troubles." He took a long pull from his beer and crushed it. "What do you call a fag with broken teeth?"

CHAPTER 17

MR. MORRIS DIED a week before winter break. It was AIDS. Those purple spots on his face turned out to be something called Kaposi's sarcoma. He'd been out for a few days last week but we all just figured he was trying to grade our essays even though all the teachers told us it was pneumonia.

The day after we found out, I was leaving band in the old half of the building and there was a clutch of students standing in front of the corpus callosum stairway. They were talking about him with the uncomfortable, awkward motions of grief of people who'd never had to express such emotions before. They were mourning not only the death of a teacher no one really liked but also the fact that they had met an honest-to-God gay person and hadn't sniffed him out.

"He seemed so regular, right?" Kevin Lawson asked. "Like he wasn't all gay-acting or anything."

Everyone nodded solemnly. He wasn't all gay-acting. Whatever that meant.

Roxanne Nolan, the kiss-ass clarinetist, said, "He deserved it. You make those kinds of decisions, do that kind of behavior, you deserve what you get."

I wanted to shove her down the marble stairway.

CHAPTER 18

WINTER BREAK FINALLY CAME. School released me to my own devices. But I just didn't have a lot of devices. Dad had bought a lot of dumb gadgets but gadgets aren't the devices the phrase means. I didn't have a lot of things to occupy my time, seeing as how I was free of friends, responsibilities, family.

The college had a film series (like an intro to film class), and they held it at the theater in town so anyone could go. If you came late you could usually miss the lecture. Tonight was *Citizen Kane*, which was supposed to be the best movie ever made. The theater was a quarter full when I showed up having run from home. It started snowing as I was running. The big fluffy silver-dollar-snowflake kind of snow. It was cold but not that cold and running gets me so hot I figured I'd be OK. It was also only two, two and a half miles. I got a small Dr Pepper to go with the two Whatchamacallits I had in my backpack. I found a seat towards the back and promptly fell asleep.

The next time I opened my eyes, the last stragglers were leaving the theater and all the ice had melted in my Dr Pepper.

In the lobby a half dozen people were stacked by the doors, shrugging into jackets, tugging at the wrist of one glove and then the other, knotting scarves in idiosyncratic magical ways—all these people performing their ritual protection dances watching the snow come down. There seemed to be some concern about the roads and it wasn't until

I got right up to the door that I saw the magnitude of the problem. There was nearly a foot of new snow just plopped down on the streets.

"Bad day for shorts," someone said behind me. It was a college kid, rocking a color-block rugby that looked like it could double as a bit of semaphore. He stuck out his hand. "I'm Brett but my friends call me Phil."

"Why's that?" I asked.

"Never asked."

"Huh," I said. "I'm Barry."

He thought for a second and responded with, "OK." His brown hair was parted on the right side and feathered and moussed into a dune of rigid fluffiness. "Why're you in shorts? Don't you have a mommy or something?"

"My mom's dead," I said, amazed at how easily the lie came out.

"Whoa. Sorry little dude." Phil looked aggrieved, mildly. "I was just making conversation."

"It's OK. It was a long time ago," I said. "I'm wearing shorts because I ran here."

There were cars spinning their tires, desperate to escape their parking spots. One of the lucky ones to get free immediately lost control on the road and slowly rotated 90 degrees and came to rest blocking both lanes of traffic. It was like watching emus ice skating—somebody was going to get hurt.

"Folks? If I could get your attention?" A guy behind the concession stand was standing on a chair and doing his best to project. He was kind-looking; he wore gray wide suspenders with brass accents. The elastic was old and curling on the edges. "I just spoke with the police and they said that no one should be on the roads right now. We need to let the plows and salt trucks do their jobs. I can't turn you all out into the cold, so we'll start up a movie again. I have a couple to choose from. We can watch *Enemy Mine* with Louis Gossett Jr. and Dennis Quaid. Roger Ebert of the *Chicago Sun-Times* gives this summary: '*Enemy Mine* is *Robinson Crusoe* set under the two suns and six moons of the volcanic planet Fyrine IV, a grim red landscape lashed by meteors and savage cold. The look of the planet in *Enemy Mine* is so convincing, the special effects are so elaborate, and the performances are so good that I only gradually became aware of what a clinker the story is.' Maybe I shouldn't have read that last part.

"The other movie we've got is *Fool for Love* with Sam Shepard and Kim Basinger. Cowboy drifter Eddie (that's Shepard) reconnects with May (Basinger), the love of his life, in a seedy desert motel, even though she's taken up with a new boyfriend, who's played by Randy Quaid. Well, it's a choice between the Quaid brothers I guess. Roger Ebert says of this one that Kim Basinger is one of those Robert Altman women characters, and I'm quoting here: 'unfulfilled women, conscious of the waste of their lives, living in backwater where their primary pastime is to await the decisions of men.' *People* magazine says that Shepard and Basinger 'ignite a sexual bonfire whose embers will haunt you.'" The man in suspenders laughed a dry hiccup of a laugh and said, "So if you want some haunted embers you know which one to choose. I guess we'll take a vote. And if you don't want to watch another movie we've got Scrabble and cards and popcorn. Or if you're sick of us all together, I called over to the Backstretch and they are staying open as well, serving adult beverages and the hermit crab racing guy is there, so good fun to be had despite the snow. And concessions is going to stay open until we go home and everything is half price. If you don't have money, don't worry about it. You can pay us later.

"Now, my wife is jabbing me with her pointiest finger telling me to stop talking but there's just a little bit of housekeeping here left. I know you all are tired of hearing from me and I am so tired of talking.

We've never had to do this before so bear with us. I'd offer up the use of the phone to you all but the lines just went down. We'll keep you all updated. As soon as we know any information, you'll know it. And if nothing changes we'll run the second movie after the first and then *Citizen Kane* once again if God forbid we're here all night. Being snowed in was not part of anyone's plan tonight, but at least you're at the movies. Let's see a VHS tape machine beat that. Now let's vote on the movie."

The movie everyone chose was *Fool for Love* first, which makes sense seeing as how they were all film nerds and it was a Sam Shepard play directed by Robert Altman, names that can make a film professor at the most expensive college in the US squeal and grunt in deep pleasure-anticipation like a pig. The movie is OK. Confusing. Kind of far-fetched. Sam Shepard finds Kim Basinger who is hiding in a hotel somewhere in New Mexico. They are old lovers. But it's not that simple. And the movie gets weirder and sadder and angrier. It turns out that the hotel is also home to their drifter father—oh right they're brother and sister, their dad is a mess of a man who never had a relationship that didn't involve him cheating.

It was over quick. Between the movies, the phone was working but the line to use it was way long. *Enemy Mine* was starting and Dad probably was snowed in at his girlfriend's and I really wanted to see *Enemy Mine*.

So here's the setup. An alien and a human end up on a planet foreign to both of them. They ended up there because they were fighting a battle in space and both of their ships were damaged. Each man was the sole survivor among his crew. Each man was stranded alone. I keep saying each man, but the alien, his race was neither man nor woman, more like both. The alien and Dennis Quaid try to fight each other then they need each other to survive and then the alien is pregnant and dying, so Dennis Quaid ends up taking the dead alien's baby to raise.

Neither of these movies were very good but I'm not sure how much I slept through either one of them. In the lobby was the college kid who'd commented on my shorts.

"You running home?" he asked.

"Do you have a better idea?"

"C'mon, my roommate has a four-wheel-drive truck."

"I'm not sure I'm OK with that."

"They're closing the theater. It's 4:00 a.m." He pointed outside; snow had remade all the parked and stranded cars into its new undulating landscape. All yellow in the sodium lights. "I'm your best option. And you know that old saying: there are no murderers in a blizzard."

"I've never heard that one."

"That's because I just made it up. Let's go. I'm right around the corner on Sandusky. We might even have some pants for you to change into."

I don't think I'd ever heard Rutherford as quiet. I could hear the snow landing on other snow. That was the noisiest thing outside of our postholing every step. When we passed the bank, I could hear the time-and-temp sign buzzing, and at the intersection I could hear the lights changing in the black box attached to the stoplight's pole. It was still snowing and the crinkle sparkle twist of the snow catching the light as it fell was the most beautiful thing I'd ever seen. My hometown was beautiful, it just took a blizzard smothering it for that beauty to be seen.

The college guy ruined it by talking. "So which one of her son's movies do you think Mother Quaid is going to see first?"

"What?" I asked, hoping that he'd not answer it.

"Her sons were in the movies we watched. Dennis in *Enemy Mine*, Randy in *Fool for Love*. Randy has the smaller role in a movie that's bad because it's pretentious but Dennis headlines a movie that's bad because it's really really bad."

"Funny," I said, immediately aware of a deep truth. "I'm sorry."

"Why're you apologizing to me?"

"It's just that if you tell a joke and someone says 'funny' after it, the joke was not funny, at all. It's like building a pool in your backyard and your friend comes over and volunteers as he's toweling off that 'it was definitely wet.' Like it's an atonal statement of what should've been obvious."

"Damn. Townie kid got some smarts. There might still be a party going on in the P&J house. But don't worry, it's like a nerd-life protection sanctuary of a house." He slapped his hand on his chest and uttered in a fancy British accent, "We are positively against the poaching of nerds within these four walls."

"How far is it?" My excitement for the snow had dwindled. My shoes were soaked and my thighs were getting chapped by the wind. I was equal parts thrilled by the snow adventure college partyness of it and worried that I wasn't being totally safe. We had made a couple of turns and I think we were near the Rax restaurant that was like a block from the quarry. I ran through all of these streets in the fall and I had an amazing map in my head of near the whole town, just no idea what any of the streets were called.

"Do you like Robin Williams? Have you seen his show at the Met? It's the fucking greatest thing that's ever skullfucked my head." Had he told me his name? Oh, right. He had. But he'd told me two names and that he was one and not the other. He seemed to be an exhausting person to be around. Or maybe I was just exhausted. "And in an unrel ted question, do you like cocaine?" He laughed hard at his own joke and then asked me if I wanted a bump.

I said, "More like a shove." Because it seemed like something funny to say and I pushed him before I saw the vial in his
hand. I realized at that moment that he was offering me drugs.
We both watched the vial get flung from his ragg wool mittens,
sparkle in its arc against the streetlights and get swallowed up by
a snowdrift.

"Why the fuck did you do that?"

"I'm sorry. What was that?" I moved towards the little bullet hole
the vial had made in the drift.

"Get away," Phil or Brett shouted. "Go in the house. Your little
chicken legs are depressing me. I'll rescue the drugs."

The house was giant. And its windows were all shining in different
colors—blue, green, red, orange. The windows of each room lit up in
its own color. I knocked but the music was so loud that it was futile.
Some screechy slow-burn music. Loud enough for a person to want
to nestle into it, like an angry beanbag chair/womb thing. I opened
the door and went in. This entry room was orange. I blinked several
times. There were several people asleep on the floor and a couple going
to town on each other on a couch by the window. And another couple
of people talking and laughing loudly who either didn't notice me or
didn't care that a stranger in shorts was hanging out in the foyer. I
could see the kitchen, a slice of harsh white light illuminating a guy
reading a textbook and smoking.

This was a campus on the verge of Christmas break. Either people
were blowing off steam or were panic-stricken over exams and papers.
Dad used to unplug the phone for the nights in the middle of December and the end of May to keep desperate students from disturbing us.
I hadn't even noticed that he hadn't unplugged the phone this year.
It's the first time ever we'll have phone service at night during the
holidays, which is good so I'll be able to reach him.

Phil/Brett banged open the door and belted out a *Here's Johnny* joke. "What's up, puppyfuckers?" His charm was built on ironic arrogance and scattershot obscenity. He'd seen too many movies about college and he claimed a BMOC role as if that was his destiny. "I brought a boy in shorts."

I didn't know who he was talking to.

"Shut the fuck up, Brett," someone shouted from upstairs.

"Ahhh, my flock speaks to me." Brett shrugged out of his jacket. He held the vial right up to my eyes. "All grains present and accounted for, I think. Unless it's all snow in there. I'm serious, it was hard work. It was like picking fly shit out of black pepper out there."

The record climaxed and ended. The silence in the house was eerie. And then the scratching sound of a needle dropped on a record and then the music. It was like being on the launchpad of the space shuttle. With your mouth open.

"What is this playing?" I was a second away from plugging my ears with my fingers.

Brett cocked his head for a moment. "This I believe is Spacemen 3. And the album, the album has the best title in the world: *For All the Fucked-Up Children of the World We Give You Spacemen 3*. We've got a guy, Trey, who spent the summer in London with his family. He picked up some weird righteous stuff over there. More shoegaze than pop."

I nodded like these words made sense to me.

Brett hustled upstairs and knocked loudly on a door. The house was massive. Brick, three stories. It'd been a mansion for one of the families who'd gotten rich off of the quarry during the limestone fad of the 1880s. The limestone barons would buy up land cheap, mine and strip the land of any charm and then donate the land back to the state for a hefty tax write-off. They made money coming and going. They brought their own workers—West Virginia mountain folk—and paid them little more than what they charged them for rent in company housing and food in the company store. The mine would eventually be spent, the workers would end up stranded and broke, and the barons built mansions. The barons founded the university, which never made sense since most of the barons were uneducated. But they founded the university to give a good education in the Methodist tradition.

Methodists are the Jesuits of the Protestant faith: they might cover up piano legs to avoid sinful urges but they also couldn't sneeze without founding a dozen schools. It was just like those early white settlers to want to set up institutions to teach the very values that they ignored in order to be successful. Maybe it was a matter of wanting more from the next generations. Maybe it was a way of smothering possible competition, slamming the door they had used to enter into generational wealth shut.

Brett opened the door and there arrayed in a loose circle was a clutch of ten people sitting on mattresses on the floor. They had a long purple bong they passed around the circle. In between bong hits, they recovered their cigarettes from ashtrays and neighbor's hands. I couldn't say the smoke in the room hung heavy like drapes or anything like that. The smoke seemed a more substantial denizen of the room than some of the students. They were dressed in ponchos and rugby shirts and cowl-neck sweaters. They wore jeans and overalls. There were ball caps advertising teams that played in different conferences and states, nothing local. Their body odor could be smelled over the stench of smoke. The light for the room was a pink harsh enough to cook the eyeballs.

"I brought us a boy in shorts," he re-announced to the group. "His name is Barry. Watch your drugs around this man."

"How is it out there?" someone in the puddle of people asked. "Is it still snowing?"

"I am sorry to announce that it is fucking snowing massively, the roads are impassable, the phone lines are down." He flopped down onto a beanbag and nearly fell over. "We need to face facts. We will run out of food soon. It's only a matter of time before we turn on each other and we'll be forced to eat each other to survive."

"Damn," a guy with a starter Flock of Seagulls cut perked up and said, "I've been eating Becca out all day and I'm still hungry."

A woman I assumed was Becca threw a pillow at the guy.

"That's your own fault," Brett said. "Everyone knows Becca is empty calories."

"Oh, fuck you. Why are you even here? Didn't you flunk out?"

Brett sat up with difficulty. His mood changed immediately— dark, defensive, and small. "I paid for these classes. I have a right to be here."

"Really? You paid for these classes? I don't think you've ever paid for anything. Your daddy, big shot at Deutsche Bank, pays for it all." Becca was clearly not ready to take any of Brett's shit.

He sat for a second, his eyes inward, his fingers tapping out a spastic tarantella on his knees. He stood up and left the room. I wasn't sure if I should follow him so I stayed in the pink room, wishing I'd had the strength to follow him out. While he wasn't my ride, he was the guy who was going to get me to a ride. This was when I started to panic. It was a blizzard, I was an easy three miles from home, and I was wearing shorts, a windbreaker, my shoes were soaking wet, and I was stuck in a room with a bunch of stoned strangers.

I was cold and I wanted to go home.

I sat there. No one paid me any attention. The bong started its journey around the room. I was brainstorming ways to refuse it when it was offered to me but I never got the chance to refuse since no one ever offered it to me. These people were only five or six years older than me but those years built an impossible wall between us. I couldn't imagine ever being their age and they had forgotten what it was like to be my age. They seemed made out of sterner stuff than I was. I was so young I was invisible.

After a good ten minutes, I left to explore the rest of the house. I went downstairs trying to find the normal fluorescence of the kitchen, with the understanding that I'd be more likely to find sober people in a room with regular lighting.

The living room was still occupied by the couple dry humping on the couch. There was another couple sitting on the floor not five feet away from the action but they were oblivious it seemed to the near-procreation happening nearby. The music was so loud that it isolated people into small clusters, each cluster its own bubble of privacy. Loud music is so much more intimate than soft music is. Soft music, you can be overheard by the whole room; with loud music the only people who can hear you are people you feel okay leaning into and speaking with your lips an inch away from their ears. The people on the floor were laughing but I had no idea at what.

In the kitchen, there were two people. A guy with half-closed eyes eating Fruity Pebbles and a woman with a book open in front of her and a pile of books next to her and a notepad, filled with the most outrageous and esoteric doodles, doodles I used to see on the chalkboard in my dad's office. I closed the door to the living room, muffling the music.

"Are you a student of Dr. Nadler's?" I asked.

She turned towards me, her eyes widening by centimeters as she took me in. "Used to be. Before he abandoned us."

"He abandoned you?" It felt like my eyes were still in shock from the pink room. I was blinking a lot and I wiped at my eyes just in case there were any tears that could be misconstrued.

She rose from crouching over her books and turned fully towards me, eager for the interruption. She had on a green cardigan which she had buttoned almost all the way up, except for the top two buttons which were missing—the little green antennas of the buttons' former anchors reached into the room probing for their lost connections. She had hazel eyes and a brilliant nose the tip of which trembled as she spoke. "The guy was the best teacher I ever had. He had agreed to be my thesis advisor. And then school starts and he disappears. No one knows what happened to him."

"I do," I said.

"What?"

"I know what happened to him."

She looked at me again. "Who are you?"

"I'm his son. Dr. Nadler is my dad. He just got a regular job in town."

"Why are you in shorts? It's Alaska out there."

"I was running and went and saw a movie. When I came out, the snow had piled up."

"But how'd you get here? It's like four in the morning."

"Brett brought me. He said someone here would drive me home."

"I thought he flunked out?"

I shrugged my shoulders. I really didn't want to get too deep into the Brett situation.

"God, he's such an asshole." She closed her book and hunkered down to give me advice. "When you go to college, don't date the first person who makes you laugh. You'll regret it. Because, you know what? That person is most definitely a first-rate clown."

I really hoped that the "he" she was talking about was Brett and not my dad.

"So what kind of job did your dad get?"

"A sales job at a manufacturer here in town. Custom containers for factories."

She looked at me like I'd said something obscene.

"Does he still do philosophy?"

I flapped my hands up and down and got immediately embarrassed by the immaturity of the gesture. "I don't think so. He's going through a whole thing with my mom right now."

"Is it your first divorce?"

"I didn't say they were getting a divorce." My eyes still stung. It was like my entire body was crammed into the very front of my eyeballs and they were threatening to overflow.

"Sorry. I didn't mean to project onto your whole thing. I've been through three divorces. I just assume parents don't stay together. We all make our armor out of the stuff that's happened to us."

"Yeah," I said. I had nothing to add to that. I'm not a deep thinker. What I wanted to ask was about somebody taking me home but I was going to start crying if I had to do something as naked and earnest as asking for what I wanted, so instead I asked, "What's your thesis about?"

"Spinoza as homosexual."

"He was gay?" The guy eating his cereal was slurping the milk. It was as loud as the music thrumming through the door. I had only eaten candy and soda for the last nine hours. My stomach was doing the irritated thing that went straight to my head and made me woozy as well as terrified that I'd have to poop. I was not going to poop there. I made a pact with my body that I'd only poop if I was at my own home at the end of all of this.

"Well, like people didn't 'come out' back then, but I think through a grammatical analysis of his diction in the German, we find that he was totally flaming. Like do you know the story of why Spinoza left the Jewish faith?"

I lied and said I didn't. We hadn't exchanged names yet. I really didn't want her to know I was named after fucking Spinoza. It just seemed too embarrassing.

"So he had these two friends, right? And they're always 'up late,' 'talking religion.' If you know what I mean."

"Yeah." I nodded like it was so like homosexuals to mask their activities with a cover story that lasted centuries and would finally be ferreted out by an undergraduate in Central Ohio.

"So they're doing their assignations. Sorry," she interrupted herself and shook her head of chin-length rusty curls so that they sproinged up and down. "An assignation is a fancy word for like an affair. It's like a sexy appointment."

"Oh. That's a good word for the SATs."

She looked at me and exclaimed, "God. You are so young. I loved high school. So free! So uncynical!" She smiled an inward smile, like she'd just found something sweet and precious inside of her that she'd misplaced years ago. "Anyway. Spinoza, right? So after he spends this time with these 'friends,' they go and tell the rabbi all the stuff Spinoza has been doing and saying and he gets kicked out the next day. And what I am saying is that he didn't get kicked out because of any heresy he was spouting, instead those little friends of his went and told them all the stuff, and I mean *all* the stuff, they'd been doing—like buttsex and oral—and they probably made it all sound like Spinoza assaulted them. So they wanted to cover their own asses by getting Spinoza kicked out."

"And there's like evidence of this, diary entries or letters?"

She deflated and sunk into her chair. "Evidence is where I'm having a hard time. It'd be so much easier if I spoke German."

"You don't?"

"This is where your dad was supposed to help translate stuff for me. He promised we were going to do this together for my senior year. And now?" She lifted her hands then dropped them on the table. "I've got nothing. I'm supposed to turn in a draft to my new advisor, who hates me but I don't want to get into it, and I have 1,500 words of an introduction and that's it."

"Have you read *White Noise*?"

"How do you think I fall asleep in this insane house? I live with a white noise machine strapped to my ears."

"No, the Don DeLillo book that came out in the fall. It's all about a professor who specializes in 'Nazi Studies,' a field he pioneered, and he doesn't speak German either and he hides it from his colleagues."

She withdrew a pack of cigarettes from a pocket I didn't know was there, took out a cigarette, tapped it twice on the table, then lit it. "Are you fucking making fun of me? You know this is my life, right? You little asshole. I should've stopped talking to you when you said Brett, Mr. King Jackass, brought you."

I tried to stumble out an apology but she'd already slapped her books closed and left.

Brett tiptoed in as soon as she left. "She's got a temper, that one."

"Were you listening in?"

"I sure as hell wasn't going to walk in when y'all were talking Spinoza. If I ever hear her talking about Spinoza again, I'll have a stroke." He held up two closed fists at my eye level. "Guess what I got?"

"I don't know."

He opened one of his hands and a set of keys was dangling from his fingers.

"Your friend let you have them?"

"God no. But he was asleep so . . . I mean I've got to get you home." He waggled his eyebrows at me. "Plus we can go and do some doughnuts in parking lots."

"Great. Let's go."

"Just a second. There are a couple of other babes stranded here at the P&J house who need a ride."

"When can we go?" My stomach contracted and I swear to God I felt my intestines—loaded with Whatchamacallits and Dr Pepper—twitch.

I decided I would tell a lie to get us on the road. "My parents are going to be really worried about me."

The door to the living room behind me opened as we were talking.

"Good," Brett said. "You guys finally came up for air. I was worried I'd have to turn the hose on you two, making out like horndogs on a stranger's couch. Shame on you."

"Baruch? Is that you?"

I turned. It was Gurbaksh and Ottilie. He was tucking in his shirt and she . . . she was radiant. My stomach got worse by about 20 degrees.

She came up and hugged me like she hadn't just had his hands all over her boobs.

"We've been stuck here all night," she said. "We came to see that band Ugly Stick play at the coffeehouse and we've been here ever since."

"How'd you get here?" Gurbaksh asked.

"I met shortpants here at the movies," Brett said. "You should've seen him when he saw how much snow had fallen. Like a wet puppy, he was either going to be rescued or thrown in a pillow sack with his littermates and tossed in the quarry. You guys ready to roll?"

"Shotgun," I shouted.

The car was a pale red Grand Wagoneer, pretty clearly an old family car that got sloughed off with the kid going to college. I had to clear all the cassette tapes off of the passenger seat. There were dozens already on the floor, which is where I put the dozen or so in the seat. My stomach didn't know who was the real enemy: the candies and Dr Pepper, Gurbaksh and Ottilie, or getting ready to drive in a blizzard with a coked-up stranger who had within the last ten minutes compared me to a puppy in a pillowcase. But I was on my way home, where my toilet was.

"Baruch!" Ottilie said. She was sitting directly behind me and she snaked her arms around the back of my seat and hugged me.

When I turned to thank her, I could only see Gurbaksh. He was glaring at me, which was kind of messed up seeing as how he had won. He got my mom and my girl, or, well, someone I had wanted really badly to be my girl. Hell, he'd even won his fight with Randy Colton. "Why in the planet Neptune are you out in this weather in shorts?"

Brett laughed. "Yeah, shortpants. Let's hear it again."

I said that I had run to the movies and that I didn't know it was going to snow this badly. I said all of this to the dashboard. I couldn't stand looking at Gurbaksh again. I hadn't seen him since the fight, a fight I was more or less complicit in. Hadn't I stood there and listened to Randy call him a 'sandnigger'?

"Don't you follow the news, dum dum?" she asked. "It's been nonstop with warnings and weather alerts. What's that guy's name?"

"Who?" asked Gurbaksh.

"The meteorologist, weather guy. On 4?"

"Jym Ganahl," Gurbaksh said. "Do you know he spells his name with a 'y'? J-Y-M. I've never heard it before."

"That's some redneck backward-ass spellings," Brett said as he rocked the Wagoneer back and forth to get free of the parking spot. The snow grunted and squeaked its frustration with us. We finally moved into the white mass of the street. "Fresh powder," Brett yelled as we inched down the street, gaining momentum. "Does this city even have a plow?"

I grabbed a tape from the floor and slid it into the stereo, not wanting to actually risk further conversation with the backseat. As soon as the first notes of a-ha's "Take On Me" played, I knew I had made a mistake.

"Oh my God," Ottilie said. "This is what we listened to that night! The one at your house? With the party? When your dad's girlfriend wanted to show us how to huff gas!"

Yes. The soundtrack to my failed date with Ottilie. The soundtrack to . . .

"This is what was playing when we first met, baby," she said, and then there was silence in the backseat which could only mean more kissing.

"Wait a second. Rewind the conversation," Brett said. "Your dad's girlfriend huffs gas?"

I tried to act like I hadn't heard him. We made a slow grunting turn onto Winter Street, one of the east-west arteries of traffic in Rutherford. All the stoplights swung in the wind, blinking their amber lights of caution.

"It's crazier than that," Ottilie said. "We almost died that night."

I shook my head and she must have seen it.

"Yes, we did, Baruch." She leaned forward and put her elbows on the center console, her head eight inches from mine. "We snuck into the garage to have some drinks, right? And this woman tags along, which was weird but it's a party and nobody really knows what's weird at a party, so we're drinking and we want to listen to the radio but Baruch doesn't want to run down the batteries of the cars, so Gurby here decides to just turn the car on."

"I'm not sure it happened that way," Gurbaksh said.

"Who the fuck is 'Gurby'?" Brett asked.

Exactly, I wanted to say. Hearing her nickname for him was so much worse than seeing them make out. I don't know why. Gurby was just awful. I was never going to get her from him if he was Gurby to her.

The Wagoneer fishtailed violently as we made the turn onto West Central and Brett was too busy turning into or out of the skid to wait for an answer to his Gurby question. The skid pushed my side of the car up on the curb. We hung up for a moment as if the car couldn't decide whether to flip over or not and then the car whoofed back down into the snow in a landing so rough the stereo spit out the cassette.

Brett gunned the car and we fishtailed some but within ten yards he was back in control-ish. We left the stereo off.

The city was eerily silent. We heard the furious ticktack of snowflakes on our windshield and the erratic muted howl of the wind. No one else was out. Not a cop, not an ambulance, not a drunk pack of college students out sledding. It was the apocalypse. We were the only living souls in Rutherford, Ohio, traveling. Just us and the snowflakes.

"I'm across from the grocery store," I said.

Brett looked for a moment like he was going to remind me that we were going to do doughnuts in the parking lot but he swallowed it. He was shook. This wasn't so much an adventure. It was something to be endured. And like it or not Brett was going to have to be an adult, something he probably chafed at in his personal life, something he probably thought was a virtue to chafe at in the past. He was in his early twenties and we were fourteen, not a learner's permit among the three of us. He had volunteered to get us home safely and now the world was daring him to make good on his promise.

"Aren't you even going to ask how I'm doing?" Gurbaksh asked.

"C'mon, baby," Ottilie said.

"No, I get stomped on by the biggest guy in school not two feet from this guy and he doesn't call me, doesn't do anything to make sure I'm fine." Gurbaksh shoved my shoulder. Then he shoved it again. "Hey, I'm talking to you."

The tears that had been promised since I'd been in the pink room finally came out, stinging my frozen cheeks. "I figured you had my mom to take care of you."

And that was that. It was too much, like cauterizing a paper cut. The car was silent.

I wouldn't say that Brett had become an adult in the process of this drive but it seemed like this was the first day he was able to conceive of himself as one, which was a little cruel considering he'd have to go home and have his parents scream at him for being such a tuition black hole. But on this drive home, the nascent stirrings of responsibility were testing whether it was indeed safe to emerge.

"You can stop here," I said. "You don't want to get stuck in our driveway."

Brett rolled up to the side of the road and put his blinkers on, which was a little much since we hadn't seen another car out there the entire night. But I liked that safety had been scared into Brett.

"Thanks a million for this. I don't know what I would have done without you bringing me home," I said, willing myself not to look at the backseat.

Brett nodded.

I said goodbye to the backseat and caught a glimpse of Gurbaksh and Ottilie holding hands. This night was probably the crucible for them as a couple. Like tempered steel, they were stronger now. I slammed the door and tried to be happy that I was home, that I could actually go to the bathroom, that I could put this night behind me. There were lights on in the house. Dad was awake. Probably furious. I'd be grounded until I was sixteen. If his anger could allow me to go poop first, I'd be fine with whatever punishment he had for me.

I was already wincing as I climbed up the porch steps. I went to unlock the door and it was yanked away from my hand.

"Baruch!"

My mother pulled me violently into an embrace. She was crying so hard that she pulled me down to the ground with her. I was still in the doorway and the wind was going to wrench the screen door off of its hinges but we stayed on the ground, my mom crying and me saying over and over, "It's OK. It's OK. I'm fine."

It'd been since the party my dad threw for himself that I'd been held by my mom and I resented how eagerly I lapped up her attention. She was holding me so tightly it was almost like she wanted to pull me back inside of her, like a fourteen-year-old fetus that wasn't done cooking yet. Half in and half outside, we hugged and cried for what seemed like forever but which couldn't realistically have been more than ten minutes.

Finally she released me, gasped at my bare legs, and asked, "Where's your father? Didn't he bring you home?"

CHAPTER 19

WE GOT A CALL the next day from the hospital. Dad had been in an accident.

When the snow started falling and he didn't hear from me he called Mom and asked her to come over to wait at home just in case I came home while he was out looking for me. He and his girlfriend got into his two-wheel-drive Corolla and latticed the town for me. He'd gone by the theater twice but never checked there. He hit some black ice on the highway, spun out, and flipped over the guardrail. Luckily a tow truck driver saw all of this and called it in before sliding down the bank and checking on them. They'd come to rest near the water treatment plant.

He had three broken ribs, a shattered femur, broken nose, a concussion, facets snapped off of three vertebrae, and frostbite on his face, toes, and fingers. His girlfriend was dead. Neither had been wearing their seat belts.

Mom and I spent the next morning shoveling our driveway. When the roads had been plowed to be passable we went down and saw him.

He started crying as soon as he saw us. His face and hands had waxy black patches from the frostbite. His leg was in traction, like one of those devices Daffy Duck ends up in in the cartoons. His head was in a halo supporting his head while the repair that had been done on his spine healed. He was broken, bloodied, infirm and it was all my fault.

My mom and I hugged him and then got scolded by a nurse for

not being careful of the miasma of tubes sprouting from him. Visiting hours were really tight in the ICU and we were shooed out after fifteen minutes. My mom and I walked silently out into the cold bright white day. She reached out to grab my hand and gripped it tightly as we found our car in the parking lot.

He was slated for at least four more surgeries and he was going to be in the hospital for nearly a month.

And this is how I got to spend Christmas break with my mom.

CHAPTER 20

FOR THE NEXT MONTH we had a ritual of visiting Dad, then going out to Chinese and a movie, and then coming home and ignoring the phone as it rang on and on.

Mr. Singh was indefatigable in his attempts to connect. There were gift baskets left to freeze on the porch (the little bottles of fancy syrups and mustards shattering in the cold), floral arrangements wilting in the winter sun (frozen orchids!), and so many messages that the little two-tape machine was topped-off with his pleading, confusion, and desire. Mom and I never talked about his messages, their relationship, or her absence. There are times when you don't want to ask if you are dreaming for the very real fear that as soon as you ask it, you'll wake up. So we played Scrabble, ate Chinese, watched movies, and ignored the little blinking light on the answering machine, flashing forlornly in the corner of the living room.

I'd stopped running. It was too cold to leave the house without gear that I couldn't afford and, now that Dad was in the hospital, had no way of procuring. Mom and Dad spent the visiting hours like they were happy with each other and had always been so. In terms of his dead girlfriend, Dad never said a word not brimming with circumspect acceptance and polite regret. Nothing is as unsettling as people who have a healthy perspective on things. The police showed up for the first week or so. And it was during one of their visits I heard my father say that her death was "regrettable." Somehow nothing seemed as awful as that. I wanted to take the opposite of a Polaroid of that moment—a memory that I wanted to instantly fade and disappear.

CHAPTER 21

THEY DELIVERED DAD'S BED three days before they delivered Dad. They set it up in the living room which struck me as wrong—he had an office, didn't he? They gave Mom and me a tutorial on the straps and buttons and cranks and counterweights and drop-down railings and bedsores and ways to make a bed when someone is still in it. The whole thing was funny.

The two guys were showing us how to recline the bed. They stressed that we shouldn't mash down hard on the button, that it was a delicate piece of machinery. But when they pushed on the button to show us how easy it was, nothing happened. It was a real comedy there as they both pushed harder and harder on the remote and it all came to a head when the nurse asked if the bed had to be plugged in. We all had a howl. And the rest of the instruction period we'd keep going back to it. Someone would say, "But does it need to be plugged in?" or "Can't pull the plug when it's never been put in in the first place" and we'd all giggle like idiots. It was almost like we were flirting with each other. Not as individuals but as groups. The two women flirting with the three men. The mother/son flirting with the technicians/ nurse. It was like the last day of camp when you meet the person you should have spent the whole of camp with.

The two men and a nurse accepted coffee before they left. The fun had stopped once we'd had everything set up correctly and Mom and I were tested on its possibilities and procedures. Now that we were all seated and supposed to talk to one another, we came up blank. I suddenly noticed that one of the men was missing his left hand (how did I miss that?) and that the other man dyed his hair (gray roots) and that the nurse smelled like the chicken salad sandwich she had for lunch. The empty bed now had a gravity and all of our best attentions were pulled into it.

It got dark but nobody moved to switch on the light. I suddenly realized that it was because of me that Dad's girlfriend is dead. I was leaned far back in my chair and I had a glass of Dr Pepper and ice against my chest. The perspiration from the glass made a damp ring on my shirt. When the two men and the nurse left it was so late that I said goodbye and shook hands with their silhouettes, their features obscured by shadows. Somebody tried a "plug" joke at the very end but it was too late, the humor too dated. The dead leaves spun in curlicues in the red of their taillights as their van dipped down at the end of our driveway and humped up onto the road.

Dad was coming home. It was real. When he came home did Mom go back to Mr. Singh? I didn't ask Mom. She didn't tell me. We'd never been a big feeling-sharing family. We worked best as planets orbiting each other.

In the dark.

And cold.

For two days, Mom and I perfected the art of walking into a room and not reacting to finding the other one in tears. I think family is just another word for the discipline of ignoring everyone's emotions and acting like everything at every moment was fine. We aspired to those crustaceans that live with their shells attached to the cliff exposed to the sea spray. Sharing the cliff, each in our own shell.

This was the best way forward.

CHAPTER 22

You wonder why people don't see it sooner but dads just ruin everything.

For example, I know this girl Margie Carrboro. We were never friends or anything. But we were in third through fifth grades together. Her dad made her sit on the stove. It left these concentric scars on her bottom. At the neighborhood pool one summer, for twenty-five cents she'd lift up the bottom edge of her swimsuit and let you see them. Supposedly for five dollars you could feel them but I never knew anybody who had that kind of money.

And then there's one of Mom's coworkers and they came over (because they were on their way to Cedar Point or something) and the daughter spilled her milk onto the dad's lap and he made her kneel in front of him and beg forgiveness in front of everyone. We were so embarrassed we didn't know where to look.

And then there was the heavy weight of Vietnam among my classmates' fathers. Some were catatonic, some were violent, some had no real filter on the shit they told or gave their kids. Kids would come to show-and-tell with bullets, land mines, and what might have been either a sprig of beef jerky or a dried human ear. Some didn't care what they taught their kids. Kids in elementary school knew how to build tripwires, pipe bombs, and how to keep your wrist supple as you performed the delicate movements to open a butterfly knife.

Some dads did damage so severe that you never heard about it.

Dads in jail, dads who hurt their kids, dads who go off to war, dads who come home from war, sullen dads, morose dads, dads and their jokes, dads and their libidos, dads who don't close the door when they shower, dads who don't pay attention, dads who sleep with other dads' wives, dads who resent their wife's success, dads who drag their son to every town Marriott has a regional office, dads who sleep with waitresses, dads who lure somebody's mom away from their kid, dads who kill waitresses in a driving accident which was in no way at all the son's fault, even though he'll feel like it was his fault forever.

Yeah.

Fuck dads.

CHAPTER 23

Mom and I were having the last breakfast alone. She'd made eggs with kimchi and bread smeared with Vegemite. Her array of exotic condiments kept most people from noticing she wasn't much of a cook.

"Coffee?" she asked with a show of brightness.

"I'll take a Dr Pepper instead, please," I said.

My mom laughed. "My dad used to drink Dr Pepper every day. He had them at ten, two, and four just like the commercials. He started drinking them to help him quit smoking and then he found out cigarettes and Dr Peppers are delicious together."

There are some people who are so afraid that they have nothing to offer that they become peripatetic, constantly moving on before anyone figures out they have nothing to give. I'm not sure what happened in my mom's life growing up (other than the broad strokes) but I think something happened which told her she was worthless inside. And while I never met either of her parents, I blame her dad. He was one of those Midwest guys who was poor before the stock market crashed so it wasn't that big of a change. He had a patchwork of at least three jobs his entire life except for during the war when he was just a soldier. My dad's mom's family had been rich and so she never recovered from the Depression. She'd been called back from her fancy New England college and ended up working at the library because that's where all of the cute guys called for dates. She made everyone know that where she was at in her life was her Plan B. Her husband, her only son, were just some things she had to grudgingly accept.

My mom's mom died when mom was in community college. She had quit to raise her younger siblings. They all got to go off to college. There wasn't money for her to go to college so she married a PhD candidate.

You marry someone, you marry their problems and their parents' problems and their grandparents' problems. You cleave generations of fuck-ups together under the guise of a religious ceremony and salt with as much hope as possible to keep the dead meat from rotting. If you thought buying a hundred-year-old house was the provenance of those who wanted to inherit someone else's makeshift patchwork solutions to load-bearing issues, you should see the people who marry other people. It's a fucking shitshow.

I heard Mom grunt behind me. Mom always had problems with opening soda cans. I took the can from her and got it open in a second.

"I remember when you had to use a church key to open those up," she said like she always said.

I sat down and took a swig.

"Oh, Barry. Could you use a glass, please?"

"Why?"

"I want our breakfast today to be special."

"Why does it need to be special?" I asked warily.

"Because your dad is coming home and I want our time together just you and me to be as special as possible. The end of our little time together."

I piled some of the eggs onto the bread and stuffed them into my mouth. It was too many flavors: Vegemite, kimchi, and Dr Pepper. My mouth felt like a strip mall's shared dumpster. I was trying too hard to make it all fit into something digestible. I spit it out in my napkin.

"You never talk about Grandpa," I said to pull attention away from my *never gonna touch another single bite off this plate* behavior.

"I don't know what there is to tell." Mom wiped her mouth with her napkin. "Well, you know he was a war hero."

"He was at Pearl Harbor, right?"

"No. You're thinking of your great aunt. No, he was infantry, a grunt. But his unit, or whatever, was recognized by name by MacArthur himself at one of his big speeches." Mom ate around her kimchi and she didn't have any Vegemite on her bread. "He went in a private and came out a private. He used to say that getting promoted when you weren't career military was putting on airs. He didn't use the GI Bill, never went to the VA or the VFW. He didn't want the government to spend any more money on an education he'd never use and he could pay for his own medical care."

"Why didn't he ever go to the VFW?"

Mom laughed. "He never understood why people would want to sit around and get drunk with each other when the only thing you've got in common is the worst thing in your lives."

She pulled a cigarette out and lit it with a tiny gold lighter that I'd never seen before. There were letters engraved on the side of it and it took me an embarrassingly long time to realize they were my mom's initials. She laughed at her dad's (I guess we'll call it a) joke.

"So he was a war hero because his unit was mentioned in a speech?"

Mom blew smoke at me and said, "You know, it's true. American kids have no respect for their elders."

"Who says 'elders'?" I laughed.

My mom blushed and got up from the table, which was an answer of sorts.

"Right," I said. "The same kind of person who says 'American kids.'" I pushed my plate on the floor, where it shattered.

"Pick that up," she said.

"Sorry." I shrugged, not unmeanly, at her. "Maybe you should get your non-American one to clean up."

"Let's not be nasty," she said to me, stabbing her cigarette out in the sink and then running water over it.

"Maybe you should find someone else to give a shit. I figured you're only here to pick up some stuff you left behind. Stuff that you want. Unlike me." I desperately wanted to walk away like they do in the movies. She could leave the family, I couldn't leave the room.

It didn't feel better to think of all the money in therapist bills I'd saved by this next little observation: The people who leave have all of the power. They can set any demands they want. "It's fine. You can love Mr. Singh more than you love me." It was the first time I'd ever said his name out loud in front of her. It was awful. I felt dirty and gross and vindictive and shitty.

Mom was facing out of the window over the sink. Her shoulders shook and let me know she was crying. "Oh shit," she said, and over her shoulder I saw the ambulance roll to a stop in the driveway. "Your father's home."

CHAPTER 24

IT TOOK THEM (three nurses) about forty minutes—clicking, one-two-threeing, and setting counterweights—to transfer from gurney to bed my father, who was in the pajamas that Mom had bought for him two days after he ended up in the hospital. It was his only pair, since he normally slept in his underwear. Mom was embarrassed that he was in danger of showing his ass to everyone, like maybe she thought people thought she was a bad wife because he was so poorly attired. There were little jars of honey in rows across a navy blue field, two sizes too big. My mom said they were the most adult pajamas she could find.

I'm pretty sure she was lying.

And when the secretary of the head of the philosophy program sent a very tasteful pajama set with matching robe ("I've been in the hospital myself, as you know, and the two things that you've gotta have in the hospital is Jesus and some nice pajamas.") he stayed in the honey jar ones.

A form was pushed in front of my mom on a thick metal clipboard. "Push hard, it's gotta go through the carbon and three copies." After Mom signed, the nurse tore a copy from the middle of the stack and handed it to her. Then in a swirl of motion the nurses were gone.

Mom stood there with the copy in her hand, like a receipt for her husband, probably feeling some sort of buyer's remorse.

Dad was trying his best, despite the pain medication, to glower at the two of us. He was angry that his girlfriend died while they were looking for me. He was angry that his wife had left him for another man. And he was angriest that he had to depend on us to take care of him. He'd been amenable while he was in the hospital, polite instead of loving. Now that he was home, he felt licensed to enact his vengeance on us.

"I need to go to the bathroom," he said.

Mom and I looked at each other trying to figure out who was going to help him out. For the rest of the year, we'd have similar staring contests. Dad's injuries had given him a leash and placed choke chains on Mom and me. Mom tried her best to be solicitous. I developed very specific hearing defects, unable to hear him or his bell. We left the TV on for him and he watched it constantly. The living room became his fort, his igloo, his quinzhee.

My dad was mourning his girlfriend. My mom was mourning her relationship with Mr. Singh. I was mourning the death of the idea of my dad as anything but an asshole.

And it was in this way that December 1985 became January 1986.

CHAPTER 25

WHEN I WAS BACK IN SCHOOL, I was hit with the news that Gary and Ottilie had run away together. Instantly they became folk heroes at school. People were coming up to ask me if I had any news, unaware of course that I hated him. When I didn't pony up any new information, the enquirer would tell me, "Thanks for nothing, Yo-Yo Fag."

Their wild adventure came to an end in the snack aisle of an Albertsons in Truckee, California. Ottilie was caught with a box of Oreos in the pouch of her anorak and the manager wasn't about to let a black girl steal from him with no consequences. The police were called. Fake names were given. Then they were taken to the police department and separated and correct names were winched out of them. Parents were called. Mr. Singh booked a ticket to San Francisco and got a rent-a-wreck for the drive up to Truckee.

When I got home I told Mom to listen to the messages that had piled up on our answering machine. The first four of them were sodden lovelorn Mr. Singh messages missing my mom, the rest were about Gurbaksh and Ottilie running away.

The problem with answering machines is that everyone within earshot hears them—it's a real design flaw. I watched Dad watch Mom listen to her boyfriend explaining how her leaving hurt him and then I watched her, studied her, as she listened to the messages about Gurbaksh, her new son.

CHAPTER 26

THE FIRST SHUTTLE LAUNCH of 1986 was on January 12.

Space shuttle *Columbia* was supposed to launch on December 18, 1985. It was rescheduled for the nineteenth because of an rpm reading that was too hot (turned out to be a bad gauge). The next shot was scheduled on January 6 but all the liquid oxygen leaked out. On the seventh the weather was crap. On the ninth the liquid oxygen sensor was broken. And then there were heavy rains necessitating a two-day delay. Everything went gold on the twelfth. Space shuttle *Columbia* stayed in space for six days and came back down safely.

Because of these delays, it was no surprise when the *Challenger* mission kept getting pushed back, but because it was such a high-profile launch due to Christa McAuliffe's presence, the pressure on NASA to get the schoolteacher in space became more and more intense. It was a cold, rainy, and windy January in Cape Canaveral. The launch was scheduled for the twenty-second. But bumped back to the twenty-third and then the twenty-fourth because of the delays with the space shuttle *Columbia*'s mission.

Mr. Singh left on the twenty-fifth to pick up Ottilie and Gurbaksh. After conversations with Ottilie's parents, it was decided that Mr. Singh would rent a hotel room at the airport in Columbus so that there could be a unified front from the parents in their lectures about Gurby and Ott's conduct. Unspoken was the idea that no one liked the idea of crying in the airport in front of all the business travelers.

The *Challenger* launch on the twenty-fifth was delayed until a night launch because of terrible weather in Senegal (the projected landing site) and then pushed back again because the secondary site in Casablanca wasn't ready for the landing. The next day the launch was postponed because ground control wasn't able to get ready so quickly for a morning launch. On the twenty-seventh there was a handle that wouldn't come off of one of the external doors.

When my mom was scheduled to go see Ottilie, Mr. Singh, and Gurbaksh on the morning of the twenty-eighth, no one really thought they'd actually launch the damn shuttle. We were all becoming attuned to the hope and delays of the space program (just as NASA was becoming re-attuned to the pressures of celebrity). And while everyone was excited for the shuttle launch, teachers were getting fed up wheeling TVs into their classrooms and then having to improv a lesson plan because of the delays. As a nation we were all grinding our teeth at night.

Let this happen already.

CHAPTER 27

THE DAY OF THE PICKUP Mom decided she wanted to bring me along for support.

And Dad had to be brought as well. He probably could've managed the few hours alone, but he was adamant that he come along. It seemed less about his physical state than a desire to stare Mr. Singh in the eyes and demand his wife back. This was all last minute so we didn't have time to recognize the inappropriateness of what we were doing.

So even though the kids running away didn't affect my dad one bit, in his present state he brought a gravity to the proceedings, the living embodiment of suffering the consequences of one's actions. He was emotional mood lighting.

Dad was out of the bed but still dressed in pajamas since they were the easiest to guide around his casts. His right leg and arm were still in their casts. The leg stuck straight out and his arm folded against his chest. Mom and I had gotten pretty good at the choreography needed to get him in the front seat and the wheelchair folded up. The music this dance was set to was my father's complaints.

"Maybe a warning next time would be nice."

"Hey, that is still attached, you know."

"Well, if it wasn't broken before it probably is now."

"I thought my last car ride was damaging."

"It seems like I'm not the only one who wishes I was dead."

We got to the hotel and Mom checked us in. The desk guy looked at my dad in his wheelchair and asked if we needed any additional assistance, but the way he said it he was letting us know that he wasn't going to help at all. And he was bothered by our presence in his fiefdom, the lobby. We were not the stylish, well-lit models in the brochures for the place. It was an airport hotel, everyone was exhausted and haggard. Except for the flight attendants. They were impeccably coiffed and aesthetically perfect for life at thirty-five thousand feet. Everyone else looked like shit.

A couple, a black man and a white woman, got up from the ochre couch and approached us. I pushed Dad to the elevator, trying to get out of their way. I am oversolicitous of black people. I need them all to like me and usually I think this is accomplished by a polite retiring away from them. And then the woman said, "Are you the Nadlers?"

"Yes? That's us," my mom said, sounding a little reluctant to identify herself as such.

"We're Ottilie's parents. I'm Rick and he's . . . No." She shook her head and put a palm to her forehead. "Sorry. I'm Miriam and he's Rick."

My parents introduced themselves and me.

"Do you all want to go up to the room?" My mom was at her best managing groups of people. "I think we all need to take a load off."

We all crammed into the elevator. I pushed our floor and exhaled loudly as if to say our journeys were difficult but soon they would be at an end. I exhaled in order to put everyone at ease, I think. Though as soon as I did it, it seemed like I hadn't exhaled in weeks. I was exhaling breath I didn't remember inhaling. I wondered where all that extra breath had been hiding.

"You're the boy who taught my daughter to huff gas," Ottilie's dad said, leaning over and into me.

"That wasn't me," I said, bouncing off of him a little.

"Who was it? Because Gurbaksh says he didn't do it either."

I fell in love with Ottilie's dad then and there, even though he looked like he was ready to punch me, punch the elevator, punch the world to get his daughter back in arm's reach. But he called Gary by his real name. There was a grace there, a kindness.

"My dad's girlfriend showed us how to do it. But nobody else actually did it. I swear, sir."

"Where's she? I want to talk to her."

"She's dead," my dad whined and started to cry.

The elevator dinged and the door opened.

CHAPTER 28

"We all become martyrs to our indecision," Ottilie's mom, Miriam, said. "A lazy manic mole-visioned set of people with infrequent fits of brilliance and rarely enough stamina to see a plan through."

We were all sitting on the edges of the two queen beds watching the preparations for liftoff. Everybody that is except for my father, who sat in his chair in the narrow alley between the two beds. We rented two rooms that have this door between them. We were all in one room because when we had both TVs on the sound was unsettling. All echo and lag.

"I don't think they're gonna launch today," Miriam said to the room. "Morons were using a hacksaw on a billion-dollar rocket just yesterday. It's too cold in Florida. We ants will have to wait for another day to build our staircase to God."

She had been narrating the launch from the moment we turned the TV on. She and her husband seemed to switch places as soon as the door to our hotel rooms closed. She became voluble and he retreated into himself.

She wasn't wrong. The launch from the day before was scrubbed because of a hatch handle that wouldn't come off the door. A bolt got stripped or something. The guys on the launchpad attacked the handle with a hacksaw. They finally got it off with a drill but not before they pushed the launch to today. It's 30 degrees in Cape Canaveral, which means that if they launch it'll be the coldest launch in NASA history.

"They want to get twenty trips this year. Twenty trips," Miriam said. "It's the end of January so they're already behind. All of our money just sitting there on the launchpad." She exhaled dramatically. "All that money for another launch that won't go and meanwhile, meanwhile, we don't have money to keep the mental hospitals open. Which is like telling all of the Vietnam vets who came back all messed up from that shameful debacle of an illegal war to go screw."

"Honey, please," Rick said.

"Don't 'Honey, please' me. Those are your comrades in arms, Rick. Your brothers. You're going to forget them?" Another dramatic exhale. "I should be the one saying, 'Honey, please.'"

"The shuttle has nothing to do with Vietnam." Rick got up and started opening drawers. "Is there coffee?"

"I saw some downstairs," I said.

Rick put his shoes back on. "All right, I'm going to make a move here. Anybody else want any?"

"They could be here at any moment, Rick. Don't go."

"I'll be back in a minute." The door slammed hard and made all of us jump. Rick came back immediately. "That wasn't me," he said. "Damn door is weird. Sorry."

He eased the door closed when he left this time.

"This has been so hard for him," Miriam said, turning an inch away from the TV to speak to our reflections in the mirror. "It's his little girl. He's a very protective father, you know. He takes her back-to-school shopping every year. I haven't bought my daughter clothes since she started kindergarten. I mean other than training bras and her other intimates. I have never figured it out but he gets so squeamish about Ottilie's developing body. Do you know when she first got her period, he didn't speak to either of us for a week?" She sucked her teeth. "He was exposed to Agent Orange, saw his buddy's head explode in a rice paddy, but tampons, panty liners, maxi-pads—those he can't deal with."

The shuttle sat on the launchpad in the early morning sun, its mighty rockets seeming to shiver with kinetic energy. They also now looked for all the world like a pair of unwrapped tampons. My insides curdled and I got a half-erection thinking about Ottilie's intimates and her periods. I resettled myself on the bed and tried to think about anything but Ottilie's underwear or about things being inserted into her body.

Miriam was still talking. "I would think he would be excited every time she got her period. Like hooray, she's not pregnant! We got her through another month!" She raised her arms above her head, making her clunky necklace and array of bangles make Boggle noises. "But no. He won't buy those things for either of us. He's delicate in strange ways. That's what I get for marrying a southerner. You know he wears all of his t-shirts inside out because the tags irritate him? I've told him just cut the ding-dong tags off. But he gives me this look like I've blasphemed the lord almighty of retail, by suggesting he take a scissor to his clothes."

There was a moment of silence in which the fact that neither my mom, dad, or me said anything made the silence have a heavier density. The silence sagged in the room. At any moment the shuttle would launch, at any moment Mr. Singh would be knocking at our door ferrying the kids home. Miriam popped the silence herself. "I mean, Rick doesn't need to buy me those things anymore. Not since I had my hysterectomy." She turned to face my mother. "Do you still have yours?"

"My what?" Mom asked, blanching.

"Do you still have your uterus?"

My dad started coughing. It wasn't that bad but I jumped up and went into the bathroom to get him a cup of water. I was hoping all of the motion of a minor coughing spell would be enough to reset the conversation.

"Hmm," my dad said when I handed him the water. My dad's mood was so down I'd need to do some major spelunking to relate to him.

The door opened and Rick came back balancing two coffees in Styrofoam cups. "I brought an extra," he said. "I know nobody asked for it but there are some people who want coffee when it's not there and there are people who want coffee when it is there." The door slammed shut causing Rick to spill one of the coffees on himself. "Motherfucker," he shouted.

"Ahhhh!" Miriam jumped up and ran into the other room. She reappeared a moment later with towels and she smothered her husband in them.

"I'm fine. I'm fine," Rick said, holding the remaining cup over his head trying to balance it while his wife patted him down. "Stop."

"Take off your sweater. I need to blot it or the stain will set." She pulled away and wadded up the towel but she saw him hesitate and she made a dumbshow of holding it up as a shield. "Don't be shy. They know about your inside-out T-shirt thing." Her movements were getting more manic by the moment. Her gestures broader, her jokes playing to some unseen audience, the Boggle noise of her jewelry more specifically emphatic.

"Stop it, dammit!" Rick tore off his sweater and shoved it into his wife's chest. "Let me be. We agreed to better behavior." He stabbed his forefinger millimeters from her face. "This is not what that looks like."

And there was an expression that flashed across her face—it looked like a ship without its barnacles, vulnerable and new and real. Not even the most sublime camcorder could have intuited it. I saw in that moment her as a girl, her as a baby, her standing outside a library alone in the rain, her so much older on a beach stabbing something curious and dying in the sand with a slender strip of driftwood. Can any of us experience another's existence without going mad? How glibly are the decisions made that change everything? These ruts of behavior that after decades we shrug at and call character. These masks we wear, letting our faces atrophy. None of this changes the temperature of the universe one bit. We are alone in the cold, cold void.

She recovered and pretended to cower, shooting us looks and doing a shaky cringe thing that I recognized as the universal pose of women in Halloween photos when the boyfriend in the Swamp Thing/ Frankenstein/Bigfoot/King Kong costume has his arms outstretched in attack.

How often do we stage our nightmares? Who would've thought the real hell was this: you and your parents waiting for your mom's boyfriend and her boyfriend's kid and her boyfriend's kid's girlfriend who really should be your girlfriend but she's not because your friend stole her from you even though you saw her first but there's also the mom's boyfriend's kid's girlfriend's parents who are melting down right in front of you. It's a long tired train of possessives to cram into a Days Inn double room. Of which let's be honest—why the shit am I here at all? Isn't there someone minding the store of my mental health? There's negligence and there's whatever I live in now.

My mom lit another cigarette with that pretty gold lighter, art deco and worn smooth. It fit in her hand so well and she enjoyed how good it felt, like, I saw her note it and smile. I'd never seen my mother as beautiful before, as a being capable of pleasure before.

My father broke his silence to wave at the air and cough.

Miriam came back to the bed with Rick's sweater in her hands. She stood up a second later and said to my mom, "Excuse me, I'm just going to scootch around you. Crack a window. I hear the smoke is bad for the heater units." She knelt down and really pushed at it.

"Hey, you're a strong young man. I have a job for you. Have I a job for you? I do!"

I looked at my mom to beg for a way out. She looked away. And took another drag.

"Scootch on down here and use those big muscles to open these windows."

I crawled down once she'd gotten up and after straining for a couple of minutes, I noticed that the windows were painted shut. I announced the fact which made Miriam beg her husband to go out and get some ice when he grumbled, "I'm just so worried about this man here, his color is just not right. I want to have some ice cubes he can hold in his mouth."

My dad was playing his silence game. And Miriam took his silence as an acknowledgement of her plan. I think my dad liked being referred to in the third person. He must've felt like it was the culmination of maturity to have people trying to guess at his needs. The wheelchair became his throne and his subjects must try their best to assuage what must be his terrible anger at the tragedy that befell him. This devotion from others was what he always wanted. Let the world service his body. He'd never felt so strongly about that flesh carapace; he wanted the freedom of his mind. He was done with translation minutiae. Now he seemed to want to commit *sati*, to be a male Dido throwing himself on the pyre of his lover's affects. But not because of the sorrow of losing my mom and then the waitress but rather because of a grave feeling of injustice, the feeling that this pain had been unjustly inflicted on him.

I really hadn't noticed before how selfish my dad was. Mom's infidelity was about him. The waitress's death was about him. His soul was a narrow hallway lined with portraits of himself.

The door slammed and we all jumped again. Rick was back with the little plastic tub full of ice.

"These ice cubes are enormous," she squawked. "How's the man supposed to hold one of those in his mouth?"

Rick kicked off his shoes and laid himself back on the bed. "There wasn't a selection of sizes, Miriam."

"I'm just worried about the man getting hypothermia." She disappeared into the bathroom and came back with a hand towel. She palmed ice cubes into the towel then wrapped the whole thing into a kind of bindle. Then she started swinging, slamming it down on the table. Bang bang bang.

"Miriam!"

"What?" She paused, already a little out of breath. "How else am I going to get them small enough for him?"

I was standing next to my mother when she leaned into me and whispered, "That woman is toxic."

For a woman who almost never cursed, this was the most damning thing I'd ever heard her say.

"Mom," I said. "What am I doing here?"

My mom didn't get a chance to answer because there was a knock at the door. It opened and Mr. Singh, Gurbaksh, and Ottilie threaded their way into the hotel room.

The three of them were exhausted and sullen. Ottilie looked wan and thin and Gurbaksh just looked so different, his face more open, his jaw more prominent, his eyes bigger and sadder. Around one of his eyes was the black and blue corona of a bruise. He looked like I'd never seen him before. Defeated.

"Gurbaksh," my mom shrieked, maneuvering through the narrow aisle between the TV and the bed to hug him. "Where's your turban? What happened to your hair, baby? And your poor eye?" The door slammed and we all jumped.

Mr. Singh shook his head at my mom sternly. The subject was meant to be tabled. This was what was making him look so different. Where his turban usually sat instead was a badly buzzed scalp. I wanted very badly to touch the thin skein of stubble that covered his head now but knew that this was not going to be possible. Gurbaksh saw my dad in his chair and looked immediately to my mom for an explanation. And that's when he saw me and the questioning in his eyes ratcheted up to astonishment. And annoyance.

"Hi, Baruch," Ottilie said. Her arms were making raising motions like she wasn't sure if we were going to hug or not. I hugged her lightly, trying my best not to have my crotch touch hers. You can never trust a penis not to get erect at all the wrong times. Even with all those days on a bus, even with all of those days without a shower, she still smelled amazing, like a mixture of gym mats and jasmine. And I wanted her more than ever and at the same time knew that I'd never have her. She was too beautiful, too smart, too wild for me. I'd never run away with her. At least not out of the county. I was never going to be able to concoct a gesture so dramatic that I'd sweep her off of her feet. She let go of me and whispered, "Has my mom been crazy?" I answered her by waggling my hand in the so-so gesture. She laughed and then went back to Gurbaksh. They were pressed against the open door to the extra room. They held hands. Resolute. My crush and my former best friend. I resigned myself to being betrayed and heartbroken. It wasn't great. At least I had a role to play though.

My dad popped the brakes off on each wheel with a loud click-thump and stiffened his posture into one of "let's go already."

Mr. Singh cleared his throat loudly. He had pulled a chair from the other room and sat in it in front of the doorway out, leaned forward with his elbows on his thighs. "It's all good. Kids are safe. We all slipped a noose here." My dad grunted out a laugh so down the ladder of utterances it could be confused with a growl. "I'd like for all of us to have a chat. We all care for these children of ours and we've worried ourselves mad during this . . . episode."

I wasn't sure if Mr. Singh was including me as one of the children who everyone cared about.

"Our families are interconnected and we need to have trust and communication, honest communication. We might not necessarily even be fond of each other." My dad nodded and said something under his breath. "As adults we need to recognize the value that we all share: our children. So let us start a conversation about what has been going on here? I have not slept much recently and I have been watching TV at night. Anything, really. I saw an advertisement that said, 'it's eleven o'clock, do you know where your child is?' " Mr. Singh dropped his head, and his shoulders shook. The crown of his turban was a geode of folds. "This advert hit me here." He chopped a hand at his chest. "Because I did not know where my child was. I did not know if I would ever see him again. I did not know if the last time I saw him was the last time I would ever see him." Gurbaksh gnawed at his lip while staring at a specific patch of the ceiling. "I do not want to ever have that feeling again. I cannot have that feeling again. If things are so bad, then we talk about them. That is what a family does. It talks."

A brief silence was broken by Miriam. She jumped up and said, "Oooooh, don't cry, Mr. Singh." She pronounced it for some reason as *Singe*. "The kids are back. We have our babies. We're not going to let go of them ever again."

"What we need to talk about is consequences," Rick said, folding his leg up on the bed with him. "Because this kind of behavior is not what is OK in our home."

"Like it's okay in ours?" my mom asked, steel in her voice.

"I don't know. I have no knowledge about what kind of whatever goes on in your house." Rick's eyes did a quick inventory of Mom, Dad, and Mr. Singh.

"Let's not go there, dear," Miriam whined.

"I'm sorry I'm not following you, Rick." My mom was staring Rick down. He'd been in Vietnam. He was a veteran. He looked away first.

"There is, how should I put this, some obvious turbulence in your house," Rick said. "I think your odd little situation—it's all a bit *Peyton Place* for my taste—is what directly caused this."

"They named their daughter Ottilie," my dad said. "But we're the ones who are odd."

"What did you say?"

"Calm down," my dad said. "Don't get your panties in a bunch."

Rick stood up but he couldn't find a way to get closer to my dad other than climbing over the bed. "You know you won't be the first person I've punched in a wheelchair."

"Do it," my dad laughed. "You can add it to my bill down at the hospital."

"I don't care what people do in the privacy of their own whatever. I do care though when my daughter is exposed to it."

"This is about our relationship? About my marriage?" my mom asked.

"What is going on in your houses is just fine, people have to find themselves." He flicked his fingers in the air. "But what I don't think . . . it's the example you're setting. Parents need to set an example."

"I'm not setting a moral enough example?" Mom wasn't going to back down.

"No," Rick thundered back. "Be married or not. Be with Mr. Singh or not. I don't care what you choose. But pick one. This is not healthy. For anyone. You can't flit around from house to house and expect either of them to be stable."

"Oh, oh, look," Miriam said. "The shuttle is about to launch."

The countdown was at less than a minute. The shuttle now seemed to shiver with energy as smoke billowed out of its idling rockets.

"Maybe we should have this conversation without the children present." Mr. Singh stood up just to remind everyone that he was tallest.

"You're the one who wanted communication," Rick said, pointing at Mr. Singh. "This looks like communication to me."

"I'm sorry. I'm sorry. I'm sorry." My mom had her fingers at her temples. "If I'm the cause of all that's wrong with this, so be it. I fell out of love with my husband. I didn't want to hurt anyone. I fell in love with someone else."

"You don't love him," my dad said.

"I do. I'm sorry but I do," my mom said.

"Fine. You love him. But you know who thinks marriage is all about love? Kids, that's who. Marriage isn't about love. It's about hard work, it's about seeing things through. It's about keeping promises, discipline."

"You make it sound like the most awful thing in the world," Mom said.

"We were due for dalliances," my dad said. "People have dalliances, flirtations, crushes. We've built something together, years of devotion, of uxoriousness."

"Does he always talk like this?" Rick asked the room. "Or is it part of his injuries?"

Now that my mom and dad seemed to be having a private conversation with all of us listening in, Miriam decided to ask us if we'd count the last ten seconds down out loud with her.

"Don't talk to me about love either. You've loved me plenty. What about when we were in Vancouver? The larches in Manning Park that autumn? You loved me then. Or that tiny town outside of Miami? The place with the burgers? And the rain? I've never loved you more than that moment."

"Here we go," Miriam clapped. "Forty-five seconds to launch."

"Yes. I did love you during those times. I loved you so much, you taught me things about philosophy and about the world, you motivated me on my career. I've done so much because of you and with you—a girl from a farm in Wisconsin couldn't even dream of. But I don't love you anymore. It just happened. Vancouver and Miami? Those were a decade ago. And I'm not a cicada, I can't burrow down and wait years and years to live again. You're not in love with me now. And you definitely don't like me. Don't pretend."

"Thirty seconds," Miriam trilled. She counted out loud and clapped her hands on every second, really expecting everyone to count down with her.

"Like you? What does that have to do with marriage?" Dad asked. "You disappear from us for weeks at a time. I have been the single parent for Barry. Do you know anything about what he's been going through? You get to do everything and I sit at home waiting for you to come back."

"It's because of me that you and Baruch have a home. You think I like living out of my suitcase? Catching flights and hotel bars? You whining about my business trips? It's all been an investment in you, in your academic career." My mom lit another cigarette. "But then, without telling me anything, without consulting with me, you abandon everything we've worked decades for. I was in love with you, I was ready to do anything for you. A PhD student while I was a lowly undergrad, you seemed full of the world and engaged with deciphering important things. But something happened, something broke inside of you, and you became something I don't recognize. I don't love this new you. I see you now and I see how much of my life I've wasted being unhappy, how much of your life I've wasted."

Mr. Singh cleared his throat loudly and said something absolutely superfluous. "Maybe the children should go into the next room."

"Yes, they don't need to hear all of this," Rick said. "I don't think *I* need to hear all of this."

"Screw you, Singh," my dad said. "You don't have a leg to stand on here. I've done some research on you and I think you need to be honest with us."

"What is he talking about?" Mom asked.

"I have no idea."

"What qualifies you to do the job you have?"

"I was offered a job. I do the job. Everyone is happy with my performance."

"But your qualifications?" My dad raised a little out of his chair, winced, and collapsed back down. "Where are your qualifications?" Dad let that sink in for a second and then continued, speaking to the room. "The schools you claim to have degrees from have never heard of you, Singh."

Mr. Singh sat back down and shook his head.

"You probably thought it was to put me in my place to get me to leave the college to be your assistant, to drive a wedge between my wife and me." The room was silent other than the TV. "But I did it to keep an eye on you, you slick bastard."

"OK, kids. You need to go," Rick said.

"Ten! Nine! Eight!" Miriam yelled, oblivious to everything going on around her. The shuttle rocked on the pad, the weight of it now suddenly obvious, its ability to unglue all of the weight from the Earth in question.

"Can't I stay and watch?" I asked.

"You should go, Barry," my mom said, squeezing my upper arm in a lame attempt at physical reassurance.

I sulked into the next room. Ottilie and Gurbaksh were sitting on one of the queen beds bent into each other, talking quietly. I sat on the other bed. The bedspreads were a riot of blotchy colors, which my mom says is evidence of a hotel that has dealt with a lot of people's blood and semen and pus, a design choice that allows the failings of the human body some camouflage. Nobody had turned on the lights, so the only illumination of the room came courtesy of the doorway into the other room, which went away completely when Mr. Singh closed their door.

The other room was noisy with yelling, the slow-motion destruction of my parents' marriage. I remembered the scene of Gatsby standing in the bushes, waiting for Daisy to come down when she never would. This is what it was like for him: in the dark, staring at a wall, some mechanisms on the other side of that wall that would break his life apart.

"Do you think we should call the front desk and complain about the noise?" Ottilie asked the room and then laughed at her own joke when it became clear no one else was going to.

Gurbaksh murmured into her ear and she peeled off a laugh that sunk me completely. It was full of intimacy. It was awful. Their little jokes. Their relationship. Who needed a wall? You could be in the same room and have no access to understanding a relationship.

"It's pretty intense in there," Ottilie said and looked briefly at me. "I'm sorry that you have to deal with this, Baruch."

"Fuck it," Gurbaksh said and reclined back on the bed. "Long as they're doing that they can't punish us."

I waited to see if Ottilie would rebuke him, protecting me. But she didn't, probably happy to realize that they were kicking a lecture down the road, probably happy to be in a darkened hotel room on a hotel bed with her amazing boyfriend.

"Are you crying?" she asked me.

I didn't think I was but it was likely. I wiped at my eyes to check.

"Waterworks is exactly what we need right now." Gurbaksh's voice had a knife edge to it, he might have picked it up on their travel out west. "You know what? Let's get out of here."

"We're already in trouble," she said with a voice that was warming to the idea.

"They," and here Gurbaksh held up his middle finger at the shared wall, "won't notice we're gone for a while. Also fuck them."

"I don't think that's a good idea," I said.

Gurbaksh stood up. My opposition to his plan made it even more urgent for him. "Nobody invited you, man. Let's go." He held out his hand to her.

"I think you should stay. They're gonna come in here any second."

"Why are you here?" Gurbaksh asked me. His shaved head was a mask, a new costume he'd put on. He was so much less naked than when he had his turban on. "No, really. Why in the fuck are you here? None of this has anything to do with you. This isn't your story at all. Bad enough we had to come back to this shitty town but you, and your dumbass dad, are part of the welcome party?"

"What happened to you out west, man? We used to be friends."

"You think I got beat up out west? Is that what you believe?" Gurbaksh rubbed his hand back and forth over his head. "This all happened here. This is the reason we left, you little shit. Your redneck friends caught up with me to get some revenge for Randy." He blinked back tears. "They beat me up and then they held me down and shaved my head. You fucking rednecks. All of you. Just die already."

He paused with his hand re-outstretched to Ottilie. She took it this time. And the two of them left, the door slamming hard behind them. I sat there in the near dark. Alone.

In the next room, Miriam started screaming. Even Rick was yelling. Even Mr. Singh. I pushed the door open and all of them were staring at the TV. Except for my mom. She was gone.

"What happened?" I asked.

"It's awful, so awful," Miriam whimpered.

I edged my way so I could see the TV.

There was a blue sky with smoke carving a giant *Y* into it.

"Where's the shuttle?" I asked, sitting on the bed.

"It blew up."

"Are the astronauts okay?"

"No way anyone survived that," Rick said.

"There was something falling," Miriam said. "Like a bright yellow hot thing falling, maybe they'll hit the water and be okay. I should pray or something."

"They're dead, Miriam."

"We should all pray."

My dad sat there motionless. I didn't realize it but he wasn't looking at the TV. This made me furious and once I started to get angry, it was like a hose being unkinked. Whhooooshh. All those astronauts dead and what was he doing? Thinking about his heartache. He should just die already.

"I am going to go fetch her," Mr. Singh said. "I don't think she knows what just happened." The door slammed.

"We should go too," Rick said, putting on his coat.

"I wanna watch this."

"Miriam, we don't know if this was an attack. We need to get home and off the roads as soon as possible." Rick slapped his gloves together and flexed his fingers. "This is a tragedy and all. But the only place I know we're safe is at home. Let's go get Ott."

Miriam pouted but stood up and started reluctantly to put her coat on. Right before she left, she hugged me, my arms pinned to my sides by the violence in it.

Rick stomped back in a second later, "Where'd they go?"

"I don't know," I answered.

"You didn't stop them?"

"How could I?"

"Your family, man," Rick shouted. "You all are fucked up. Stay the hell away from me and mine from now on."

Bang, the door slammed.

My dad and I stayed in the room. Me staring at the *Y* in the sky, him staring at the drapes.

"It's my birthday," I said to the TV. "I almost forgot. I'm fifteen today."

My dad grunted.

He sat there staring. After a half an hour, I turned off the TV and left.

The door slamming behind me.

THIRD PART

"The house of pain and disease has been demolished.
The men and women celebrate."
—*Guru Granth Sahib*, Sorat'h, Fifth Mehl

HATE IS SAFE. Hate is urgent. Hate is unkind. Hate is ubiquitous. Hate singles the hated out and provides anonymity for the hater. Hate is comfortable. Hate tells the hater that they never need to change, that they have special sight into the failed world, that they are justified in hating.

Glorious and holy circular logic of hate.

Hate gives us friends but since the basis of friendship is hate, each person will be wary of the other. Communities of hate form quickly and dissipate quickly, looting one another of our emotions, leaving traces of themselves everywhere while everyone involved claims they're blameless. Hate makes us lonely. Hate plus time ossifies us into that loneliness. We all die alone. Hate helps us realize what death will be like, so when death shows up, people who've spent their lives hating will recognize it for what it is. Hate is a coffin buried six feet in the earth, sealed away even from all the other dead. It'll take decades before the first worm breaches the ornate lacquered wood and finds its food. Hate is rage and sadness and vengeance given voice. Sometimes hate acts like it's the only thing left to trust when your world falls apart.

I was in a daze for about three weeks after what happened at the airport Days Inn. I dropped out of school because I was having a hard time getting out of bed. I was too young to drop out so my dad told them that he was homeschooling me, which was true I guess. He had taught me a lot recently.

I got a job at a little motel in town and got paid under the table. I painted parking blocks, I rewired lamps, I patched walls, I studied for the GED. I stopped seeing people my own age. I hung out with Jim the main maintenance guy who told me that cigarettes aren't what caused cancer rather it was what was in matches that was the problem. "That's why I always use a lighter." And the women I saw everyday creeped into my fantasies, a trio of middle-aged women employed as maids.

Once Dad was out of his chair, he and I came to an agreement. He cosigned on an apartment for me and I moved out for him. We never talked about what happened that day in the hotel, whatever was said between the launch and the explosion I'll never know. And I think he felt that getting me out of the house would prevent that conversation from ever happening.

Since I didn't go back to school, I didn't have to turn in my project on the *Challenger*. I did though learn a lot of jokes from Jim about the *Challenger*.

What was the temperature of the ocean after the *Challenger* exploded?

Seven below.

What did Christa McAuliffe say to her husband before the launch?

You feed the dog, honey. I'll feed the fish.

What I realized about the jokes, even though I hated them for a long time, is that they serve to callous up the sensitive parts. And maybe that's what was going on with all of the gay jokes too. As the body count of AIDS rose higher and higher and we all got a sense of how awful the disease was, the jokes took that nascent empathy with the afflicted and smothered it in its crib. Like we could maintain a sense of how the world should be by leaning into our hatred and mockery of the diseased and dying. Jokes provided some kind of handle on our emotions, helped make some sense of the damned carnival chaos of existence. We could control the world by slotting it into setups and punchlines.

What were the last words said on the shuttle?

No, I said a Bud Light.

Where did Christa McAuliffe spend her vacation?

All over Florida.

They came back and said the causes of the explosion were the O-rings and the cold weather. There were congressional hearings and everything. The shuttle was shelved for a while. The twenty-two planned launches for 1986? Gone. The program for civilians to go up into space? Shelved. There was this moment before the explosion when we had a future all set for ourselves and we were trundling towards a space-age utopia—flying cars, jet packs, people on Mars, international space stations. And then it was gone. Replaced by a giant yawning Y in the sky. Mom and Dad divorced. Mom and Mr. Singh married. Dad got Mr. Singh fired for not having his degree.

What color were Christa McAuliffe's eyes?

Blue. One blew this way one blew that way.

There's a distance between what we think will happen and what does happen. And those of us living in the fallen world, post-explosion, make jokes designed to desensitize ourselves to the death of our dreams.

What does NASA stand for?

Need Another Seven Astronauts.

It's like we need to resort to greater and greater grotesqueries in order to keep us from crying all of the time. Mom and Mr. Singh moved away to New Hampshire. They sent me cider doughnuts in boxes with love notes stained with grease.

Did Christa McAuliffe have dandruff?

Yes. They found her head and shoulders washed up on the beach.

No one leaves this world unsullied.

They knocked down the house where Rutherford B. Hayes was born. They put a BP station there. And a plaque to commemorate what they knocked down.

The past can be erased as well as the future.

LAST PART

"You know where you are? You're in the jungle, baby.
You're gonna die."
—Axl Rose

JUNE 1991.

It was the week before high school graduation and Gurbaksh had come for a visit. We'd done some patching up over the years, done some Christmases together, even saw Blues Traveler together which made no sense at all since neither of us could stand jam bands. Maybe we'd done it to have some people we could laugh at together again.

"You're my only brother," he said when I asked why he was coming to visit. "I miss you."

But I had the sense that he was coming for Ottilie rather than me. She was at Oberlin. And we were going to drive up and visit her after this weekend. "Reunite the team supreme!" he said. He was anxious, kind of perpetually zipped up. He was always talking about that semester of high school we'd spent together, remembering parties and teachers and madness. He still wasn't wearing his turban.

"I've had an anti-religious conversion," he said. His black hair was chin-length and he was forever pushing it back behind his ears. He was beautiful.

I was twenty years old and working at Honda of America. I was in Post-Weld. The raw-weld bodies of Accords drifted towards me on these massive hangers. My job was to put spacers on the doors and bars to secure them, so that when the weld bodies were dipped in the electrolyte bath the doors would stay securely ajar, allowing the bath to coat everything. It's all about getting the paint to adhere more securely or something. I'm kind of notorious for reading during lunch.

Gurbaksh crashed on the couch and stayed up late watching my videotapes. I'd accumulated kind of a lot since I'd been taken on full time at Honda. I've never had this much of my own money before. O'Dell, my shift supervisor, keeps at me to reapply to colleges. He likes my work and all but he wants me to go to school, says he doesn't want to see me wait twenty years for retirement before I live my dreams. I tell him going to school doesn't always realize everybody's dreams. He tells me he hates to see brains go to waste.

You know who works there? It took me a month or so to recognize him but it's Trevor, the bartender. He's in charge of replenishing our parts bins. He's terrible at it and he gets a hell of a time from the other guys for being late and sloppy. He's a little shelled out, more residue than man at this point. I'd say he doesn't recognize me, but he doesn't really see me, doesn't really see anybody. Some people weren't built for Plan B living.

I told all of this to Gurbaksh. He told me about his classes in Medieval Literature, Statistics, the Old Testament, and Intro to Sculpture.

"There was this time last February, I shit you not, when all of my classes started bleeding into each other. Like I was seeing connections between them that I don't think anyone had ever seen before." His eyes were bright with fervor as he smoked this pack of cigarettes I had lying around and ashed into an empty Keystone can, whose slogan "Bottled Beer Taste in a Can" suckered me into buying a six-pack. "It's the closest thing to like the spiritual, I've ever experienced."

"What's your major going to be with classes like that?" I asked.

His eyes cleared up and he looked so disappointed in me. "I don't have to declare until the end of next year, Dad."

He gave me a look like I was just another one of those people who just didn't get it. And he was right, I didn't. Here I was making $32K a year and he was pissing away my mom's money so he could have pro-found connections between sculptures, scripture, and math problems.

"You're not even wearing your *kara* anymore?" I asked.

"It's creepy that you both noticed and know the name of my bracelet."

"First thing I told you when we met was that I had a library card."

"And you're not afraid to be obnoxious about it." He tucked his hair behind his ear. "I think I'm done with it all. I realized that while Sikhism is the best of a bad bunch in terms of religions, I just couldn't subjugate myself to a religion with a dress code." He lit up another cigarette. "I'm gonna borrow your car, OK? It's still hard to believe that it's your car. I can't believe my dad gave you his Saab."

"I bought it. He sold it to me."

"For like five hundred bucks. I should've gotten the chance for a competitive bidding process." Gurbaksh sulked.

It was a deal, but the brakes were shot and it needed a new transmission and the only person who would work on it was in Columbus and booked to judgement day. I did like driving the red Saab around, even though all the guys at Honda gave me endless amounts of shit about it.

"Whatever," I said to his aggrieved face. My mom was putting him through school and his dad gave me a deal on a used car and somehow he was the wronged one. Some people don't know when they have everything already.

We were supposed to go up and visit Ottilie that weekend and right around the time when we'd run out of things to talk to each other about someone had jammed a flier for a graduation party in my apartment's mailbox, "Bonfire Down at the Quarry!" I'd barely spent any time at the damned school but they must've still had me on some inalterable mailing list. I threw it away immediately, but when I got home on Friday Gurbaksh had it smoothed out on the dining room table.

"We should totally go to this," he said.

"I thought we were going to Oberlin," I said, peeling off my steel-toe boots. My downstairs neighbors had complained about the clomping so I took them off when I came home.

"Ottilie has some end-of-the-year dinner thing going on tonight," he said. "This will be hilarious. We'll be some real throwback, blast-from-the-past guest stars."

"I'm not sure, man. I bump into a lot of these people around town enough as is." I opened up a beer and cracked a window. Gurbaksh had run through my pack of cigarettes and picked up another pack from the United Dairy Farmers on the corner. "None of them has changed."

Last August, we invaded Iraq. The city was littered with Support the Troops car washes, pancake breakfasts, raffles, and candy sales. The Vietnam Vet dads seemed to be overly amped up about the fact that we should be supporting our troops. It was like they were admonishing the rest of us for not supporting them back in the day.

I hadn't been called Yo-Yo Fag since I quit school. Saddam Hussein and this war—it's like everyone found someone else to hate.

"But we've changed, man." Gurbaksh opened a beer as well and pushed his hair behind his ears before he drank. "Let's go rub our success in their faces."

The party was at Blue Limestone Quarry in the center of town. I hadn't been to a high school party since my disastrous freshman year, but even though I had no real friends and I hated everything about high school I got suckered into Gurbaksh's nostalgist zeal. So I put on some sweats.

Blue Limestone Quarry had playground equipment, baseball diamonds, and a picnic shelter. The quarry had been filled with water from a diverted stream and even though there were "No Swimming" signs posted everywhere two or three people drowned there every year. There weren't any directions on the invitation because no one would need them. The bonfire was almost visible from my apartment. We followed it like a thousand other moths that night.

"When did you start smoking so much?" I asked. The air was brisk for a night in June and I wish that I'd worn a jacket. There was a moldering smell of cut grass that nearly choked me.

"This is crazy, right?" Gurbaksh said. "Do you think anyone even remembers us?"

"Maybe," I replied, feeling like it probably went without saying that turban or no, Gurbaksh was going to be remembered. I'd prefer no one remember me from those days.

"Do you think we could get lucky? We should set up a signal just in case one of us is going to get lucky." Gurbaksh was already three beers deep into the six-pack that we brought.

What about Ottilie? I wanted to ask. There was nervous energy peeling off of him as we walked. Something had happened between the two of them. I was getting that Gatsby in the bushes feeling, staring at the wall waiting for someone to give me answers. At this point, I'd be surprised if we ended up in Oberlin at all that weekend.

The fire was about two stories and it hurt to look at even from a quarter-mile away. There were layers of party, like concentric orbits around the bonfire. There were kegs sprinkled on the edges, minor moons which had their own weaker gravitational pull of boys and girls impatiently chugging beer from plastic cups brought from home. The outer edge of the party was owned by the pot smokers. Then the stumbling asteroid field of drunks moving erratically, powered by their hilarity, arrogance, and solipsism. There were minor bands of dancers surrounding ghettoblasters pumping out Metallica, Aerosmith, Guns N' Roses, Naughty by Nature, and Digital Underground. Then there was the band nearest the fire: full of sad drunks staring into the fire as if that's where the answers were, high glassy-eyed gurus overwhelmed by the heat and spectacle, couples making out, the same foursome who played euchre every lunch period my freshman year was here with a card table playing euchre. You almost couldn't go anywhere in Rutherford without seeing people playing euchre.

Gurbaksh peeled off from me and went to hang out by the kegs. He was drinking a lot. Maybe he was figuring out what a bad idea this was.

"Little Psycho!" Randy Colton put his arms around my waist, half hug, half wrestling move—showing his affection and his dominance at the same time. "Fuckin' perv. How are you?"

"Hey, man. How've you been?"

"I'm graduating, man. Who would've thought this burnout would ever get it together?" He cuffed me on the back of the head. He was a high school graduate at twenty-two. It was good to see Randy so nakedly elated. I was proud of him. "Look at you, Barry. You grew. You're like the size of a regular person now."

"Yeah. Puberty happens." I smarted a little at this. Compliments wrapped up in punches or the other way around—men don't communicate any other way. "Even to us Little Psychos."

"Hey, man. I never got the chance to thank you for being so cool about not telling anyone about catching Holly and me fucking."

"Who would I have told?"

"Yeah, it was still cool of you. Porky would've had my nuts for that one," he said. "You heard they got married right?"

"Whoa."

"Yeah, they're already divorced." Randy's eyes danced with glee at his cousin's misfortune.

"That was fast."

"Can't trust women, man." Randy blew some snot out of his nose onto the ground, hard. "Hey. Do you want some doses?"

"What?"

"LSD, man. You wanna trip?"

"Oh. I didn't bring any money." This wasn't true. I had fifty bucks in my sweats. But why was I not saying *No*? What door was I opening by not saying *No*?

Randy rubbed his chin and said he'd give it to me as a graduation present almost like I knew he would. I am not sure but I think I just manipulated a redneck into giving me free drugs because I also still hadn't told him I'd had my GED for three years now.

"What's this going to be like?" I asked as he opened up his wallet and pulled out a folded cigarette cellophane with scraps of blotter paper in it.

"You've never done it before?"

"I've heard it like makes you hear colors. And jump off buildings." I held the little rectangle of paper up to the firelight. "Will it make me an asshole?"

"Put it under your tongue. Let it dissolve there. It, like, makes you more you, you know? Like you only a lot more."

"It doesn't taste like anything. You sure I got some?"

"This is so exciting. Doing acid with Yo-Yo Fag." He clapped me on my back then punched me in the gut with his other hand. He leaned in close to my ear and grunted out, "It is good to see you, Little Psycho."

Dear God, when *Appetite for Destruction* was released in 1987, it didn't seem as much new as something pure vomited up from the subconscious of the Midwest wrapped up in the tinfoil of hair metal and jammed into the microwave of Los Angeles. See, when Axl Rose first started jitter-stop high-stomping around the stage, any Midwesterner worth his corn recognized him as one of our own. Axl was from Indiana. He got out. He left and he found the streets lined with cocaine in LA. This was our collective fantasy. To leave.

If I left, and I made a whole new life for myself somewhere like Texas or Maryland and I ran into someone from my high school would they be my kryptonite or would they be more like a phantom limb that finally got itched? Axl was weaselly white trash and here he was being treated as a sex symbol. There was a revolution at work: the half that has always felt like shit because the rest of the world seemed to run on greased rails realized that life was always going to be a slog patching together jobs in order to stay ahead of the creditors and out of the range of what passed as justice in a neighborhood left by the city to go feral for lack of property tax revenue. And that half of the population decided to just get high and watch it all burn down. Like a lower-class nihilism. Everybody gets all bent out of shape about NWA and how they glorify gang life but it's Guns N' Roses we should all be watching out for. The sludgy pumps of their malformed hearts will drown us all with their talk of blood purity and heroin. This is what we've empowered—not Rodney King but the cops' fear and glee as they wailed on him.

I was at the fire sitting on an old tire, wondering when the acid would kick in. I might have gotten a dud. It was nice sitting at the fire on an old tire. Fire. Tire. A fired tire is better than a tired fire. It was really impressive how they got the fire to dance to the music.

Randy bumped me over and sat down on the tire, handing me a beer. "Where'd you go? I went around the party three times looking for you."

"I've been here," I said, pointing to the tire. My throat was so dry, I drank what must have been half of the beer before I remembered I hated keg beer and spit it all out back into my cup. "Right here, for as long as I can remember." I paused to listen to a secret the fire was telling me. "I think the drugs are kicking in."

"So your boy's here." Randy punched me in the arm. "Back from college or whatever."

"Who's that?" I asked but I knew he was talking about Gurbaksh. There was literally no one else that Randy would be talking about as "my boy."

"Your shit-brown friend. The one with the turban." Randy took a big swig out of a silver flask and offered it to me. "The one whose ass I kicked."

"Nice flask," I said, taking it from him and sniffing the tip of it. I took a drink and my sinus cavity felt like it'd been napalmed. I gagged and coughed and wheezed then I took another drink.

"Except he's not wearing the turban anymore."

"What?" I asked with snot dripping out of every orifice on my face.

"He's not wearing his turban. He's got some bullshit faggot grunge haircut."

"Yeah," I said. Whatever bad blood still existed between Randy and Gurbaksh I wanted no part of. "I thought I saw him."

"He's still some type of Saddam-worshipping oil-rich camel jockey."

I rubbed my eyes with the hem of my shirt. "You know he's not a Muslim, right?"

"Fuck you."

"He's a Sikh."

"Is that like Sunni or, what's that other one? Shih Tzu?"

"No," I answered, amazed that Randy knew so many sects of Islam. And dog breeds. "It's a warrior culture from India. It's a mixture of Hindu, Islamic, and its own teachings. It's a beautiful religion. The next time you're in a library you should check out a picture of the Golden Temple in Amritsar on the border of Pakistan and India." I wondered if the Rutherford County Library ever replaced the world religions book that I tore the Golden Temple picture from. I was such a little faggot about Gurbaksh when I first met him.

"You know what Muslim means?"

I didn't. I was disappointed in myself. Or maybe I just wanted to hear what Randy thought it meant.

"To submit." Randy poked me hard in the chest with each syllable.

And he said it again as if I were going to miss his point. Which I was. "To submit. So you're not just fighting people—a person has a brain and like free will. What we're fighting now—damn." He spit a fine stream of tobacco juice in the direction of the bonfire. "It's like nigger commies but with religion. We should just nuke that whole area until it's glass. Cigarette?" He shook his pack at me. It drifted in rainbow waves for so long that I took one just to make it stand still. Randy lit it for me and stuck it in my mouth, laughing and pounding my back as I choked on my first inhale.

I wanted to get out of there, grab Gurbaksh and get back home. My legs weren't working though.

Randy pulled a folded-up piece of paper from his jean jacket. "Have you seen this? Fucking hilarious but it's got like a real point, y'know."

The picture was clipped from a newspaper and was drawn in the "political cartoon" aesthetic. It showed a man wearing white robes and a turban. His face was a grotesquely "Arabic" caricature—giant nose (complete with profuse nose hairs), bushy eyebrows, massive beard, wildly furious manic eyes. He was swinging an enormous sledgehammer intending to slam a camel's hairy testicles which sat on a tree stump in front of him. The camel, who was sweating profusely, had an enormous missile shoved down his throat so that only the tip and the first set of aerodynamic fins were exposed. The picture was titled "Iraqi Missile Launcher."

I wondered what was the "real point" Randy found in the picture. That Iraqis were technologically backward? That they were so willing to fight that they'd sacrifice their camels' fecundity for their home-land? That Iraq was a country so beneath the United States in terms of military power that they were easy pickings? What was the artist's reason for drawing this limpid scrap of propaganda? Why would a newspaper run it?

My stomach felt dry and heavy. My eyes were doing a weird thing. I was blinking like crazy.

I folded the paper and gave it back to him. "But you know that Gurbaksh is not a Muslim, right?"

"He's part Muslim. That's what you said." And that's when I saw all the guys standing behind Randy. I could've sworn one of them was the one I'd seen beating his dog all those years ago. Still shirtless. Still in cutoffs. Like a Dickensian ghost of some lower caste's anger. "It's even worse. Some half Muslim who worships gold." He spit on the ground.

"No. I said 'Golden Temple.'" I asked, "Who are they?"

"Don't worry. They're all family," Randy said, then burped. "Patriots."

Stoned, confused, a little drunk, I'd been garrulous about the Sikhism stuff, trying to impress Randy with how smart I was. They were a crowd of hillbillies on acid and what I said to Randy was flash-fried into what they wanted it to mean.

I was just one small-for-his-age guy. I had been bullied so much, so long, and so often that I didn't notice that what I said matters. No one ever listened to me. Why did they start at that point? Since when did my words matter at all?

"There he is," someone said, and the crowd of four or five guys snaked its way towards Gurbaksh. I saw him smiling, a brief flash of his full-fledged drunk charm. He tucked his hair back behind his ear. I should have told him to run.

Randy and the rest of them circled Gurbaksh and at first I thought they were just talking. Randy had his arm around his shoulder and Gurbaksh had his around Randy. They could've been mistaken for friends. I saw Gurbaksh give Randy a cigarette, then while he was lighting Randy's cigarette, someone brought a beer bottle down on Gurbaksh's head. He swung around and then the shirtless guy punched him hard in the stomach. Gurbaksh basically hung on the guy's fist and soon the other guys started punching him, knocking him loose and once he was down on the ground, they kicked and stomped him.

I turned away and groped in the moonless dark, looking for an escape. As chants of "USA! USA! USA!" filled the air, I struggled in the night to find the ruts of the dirt road and once I got onto it I ran. By the time I got to Houk Road, I couldn't ignore the screams any longer and cars started to pour out of the party careening in all directions, like marbles scattered on a dance floor. I was tripping from redneck LSD and all of the headlights bouncing over the ruts made me nauseous. I ditched the road and ran into the woods. Briars reached out and grabbed me, tripping me, scratching me. I stumbled in the crick but kept running. I heard screaming and I heard sirens and in my head, trying hard to separate scream and siren from scratch and wet, there was a fuse that burned out.

The police found me in the morning. And they were so distracted and glum, I knew my sleeping out in the woods wasn't the tragedy here.

As there wasn't a *gurdwara* nearby, it was a simple funeral in the Methodist church. But it was like the whole town had turned out for it. There were cops on hand to make sure there was no more violence and also to show that law and order were present even if they were more often than not late. Randy and the other Coltons involved in his death were in jail and everyone felt a little too good about that, as if them being caught absolved any of the rest of us.

Mr. Singh was going to read the entire required forty-eight hours from the *Guru Granth Sahib* himself when he was back in New Hampshire but had pulled a small selection out to read here. He couldn't get through it and he was crying so hard that for a while no one went up and comforted him. He scolded the town with his grief and we all took it into our hearts as deeply as we were able. His tears echoed in the big chapel.

And outside of his weeping, there was silence. The entire chapel filled with people and no one moved. All there were shamed by what had happened, what had been allowed to fester in their town, in their hearts. And I was proud of their shame. I saw their earnest shame, people for whom earnestness was all they had to shield them from the world, and I knew it meant something in that moment, even if it would mean nothing an hour after the service. I was ashamed. I was one of the chief mourners and at the crucial moment, I'd done nothing but run. So worried about getting punched or called a nasty name that I let someone else die instead.

I was a person skilled at transmuting my sins into virtues, who exemplified cowardice but believed it to be restraint, a cynic who called it rational thought, a possessor of a broken and closed-off heart, who blamed others for its failures.

We all sat there and listened to him cry, just as they had all stayed silent when I was bullied, just as we had stayed silent as the Coltons killed Gurbaksh. The Coltons were a minority in our town, evil was a minority in our town. But the majority lived in a tepid silence, avoiding the difficult confrontations, avoiding standing up for each other. I hated their silence the most. I hated them.

Mr. Singh stopped crying and sat down and everyone felt relieved to be let loose of a feeling too close to complicity to bear. I felt as bad as I could at that moment, but what was worse was that I knew I'd forget this moment, that time would erase this pain.

See, I was always going to be safe. I was not a survivor because of some inner quality of strength or courage, which at this point can surprise no one. I was a survivor because I learned how to hide, learned how to stand to one side when the evils of the world came down, hoping they'd attack anyone else but me. Lucky for me, hiding was possible. I blended in. Unlike Gurbaksh, I looked like my tormentors.

The service ended, and the town filed out. Gurbaksh was to be cremated and Mr. Singh wanted his ashes spread in the crick near where he had died as a rebuke to the town that killed his boy. But in the meantime, my dad opened up our old home where he now lived alone and hosted a potluck of mourners. The dining room table groaned under the weight of the dishes. Before anyone got there, I had to run through the house and hang "No Entry" signs on the rooms Dad had ceded to the invading wasps. I tried to busy myself with these dumb tasks.

I stood on our front lawn, pointing out where people should park. Ottilie came up to me and said something but I was too dug down into myself to hear it. She was with some guy, like I think she brought a date to her old boyfriend's funeral, and maybe it was this guy who was the real reason Gurbaksh and I never went up to Oberlin. And maybe she felt as awful and responsible as I did. But it didn't matter. Even if we felt awful, we still got to feel something, while Gurbaksh was . . . beyond any kind of feelings. I hated that I got to keep on living.

For the majority of the reception, I paced around outside my father's house. To go inside even to pee felt awful. All those people and their mouths being stuffed with food from plates balanced on their knees, it was grotesque. The stink of grieving: talcum powder, dry cleaning, and well wishes. The humanness of it all. This was the obscenity of Gurbaksh's death. That we got to continue. That we got to "draw lessons" from his death. I kicked over an anthill and suppressed a wish for matches.

People lingered. People left. I helped them find their jackets, wrote down names on Post-its I attached to their Pyrex dishes to return later, accepted their apologies that they couldn't stay later, and aided while they navigated their cars from our lawn. I stood on the front lawn and stared at my house, with my father, my mother, and stepfather inside. I was amazed that this house had been able to stand for over one hundred years. It seemed an insult to gravity.

I knew there was goodness in this town, that there was goodness in me, that goodness was possible. But it would always arrive too late, bearing overcooked casseroles that no one would eat. I hated Ohio for what it had done to my friend. I hated it for what it had done to me. I hated myself because the only strategy I was any good at was escape.

After everything was cleaned up and final hugs handed out to Mr. Singh and my mom at the airport, I climbed into the red Saab—packed with all of my books, half of my clothes, a lamp—and left. For good.

ACKNOWLEDGMENTS

I WAS BULLIED IN SCHOOL. Even worse, I bullied other people. It's the friction between bullied and bullying that this book came from. The problem of not feeling loved by my community was compounded in me by the guilt of not loving, of not knowing how to love my community. There's something there but when I try and put it into words it slips away. That's why I had to write this book.

Big thank-yous to Tracy Carns, my editor, and to Stephanie Kip Rostan, my agent. Both of you saw something special in the early drafts, and I thank you for your belief in me.

Thank you to the men I got to work with in Division 10 of the Cook County Department of Corrections. Your bravery and vulnerability helped me as I wrote this book.

Thanks to Noname, whose albums played constantly as I wrote. Same goes for Spiritualized, Chance the Rapper, De La Soul, Bobby "Blue" Bland, and Ugly Stick.

A big thanks to my sister Katie, who's always up for reading a draft and talking about music and movies and soul stuff. Thank you to my sister Betsy, who more than once defended me from the bullies of my hometown.

Scott Brown is a fantabulous writer of things from TV to Broadway to books. He's amazing and one of the best texting friends I've ever had.

Thanks to Gillian and Brett, readers extraordinaire and dear friends.

Thanks to Scott Repass who dropped what he was doing and flew out to help me and my family when my depression got as bad as it could get. He's the greatest in so many ways. Friend. Writer. Bar owner. Parent. Husband. Human.

Thanks to my totally excellent in-laws, Susan and Errol Stone.

Thanks to my wonderful parents, who support me even when I write things they don't like.

Thanks to all the mental health professionals who've kept me in this world when my brain chemistry wanted otherwise.

Thanks to my kids, who make every day a whirlwind of blessings and chaos.

And to Emily: best reader, best partner, best friend. I've learned more about love than I ever expected to learn. Thank you.

Islamophobia, homophobia, and racism are all part of this book; sadly, they are defining parts of American culture as well. People who want to know more about how to combat these ills in schools can go to It Gets Better (itgetsbetter.org); islamophobia.org; Islamic Networks Group (ing.org); and sikhcoalition.org.